Indiana
State Facts

Nickname: Hoosier State

Date Entered Union: December 11, 1816
(the 19th state)

Motto: The crossroads of America

Indiana Men: Larry Bird, *basketball player*
James Dean, *actor*
Michael Jackson, *singer*
David Letterman, *TV host, comedian*
Cole Porter, *songwriter*

Flower: Peony

State Name's Origin: "Land of the Indians"

Fun Fact: Indianapolis Motor Speedway is the site of the great sports spectacle, the Indianapolis 500.

My New Mommy
BY
Sarah Bartholomen
age 7

When I was borned my mommy had to go to heaven but Dr. Merry made Sure I was oK for Daddy.

When I was little last year Merry comed to see us all. Me and Jared and Daddy liked her. Then we loved her. She loved us.

Its a long story. She married Daddy. We are all glad.

American

HEROES

AGAINST ALL ODDS

CELESTE HAMILTON

A Fine Spring Rain

Published by Silhouette Books

America's Publisher of Contemporary Romance

For fellow writers—
Wanda Blankenship, Anne Doggett,
Tawnee Kirby and Opal Privette.
Thanks for your help.

SILHOUETTE BOOKS
300 East 42nd St.,
New York, N. Y. 10017

ISBN 0-373-82212-X

A FINE SPRING RAIN

Copyright © 1989 by Jan Hamilton Powell

This edition published by arrangement with Harlequin Books S.A.

® and TM are trademarks of Harlequin Books S.A., used under license.
Trademarks indicated with ® are registered in the United States Patent
and Trademark Office, the Canadian Trade Marks Office and in other
countries.

Visit Silhouette at www.eHarlequin.com

Printed in U.S.A.

About the Author

Celeste Hamilton has been writing since she was ten years old, with the encouragement of parents who told her she could do anything she set out to do and teachers who helped her refine her talents.

The broadcast media captured her interest in high school, and she graduated from the University of Tennessee with a B.S. in Communications. From there, she began writing and producing commercials at a Chattanooga, Tennessee, radio station.

Celeste began writing romances in 1985 and now works at her craft full-time. Married to a policeman, she likes nothing better than spending time at home with him and their two much-loved cats, although she and her husband also enjoy traveling when their busy schedules permit. Wherever they go, however, "It's always nice to come home to East Tennessee—one of the most beautiful corners of the world."

Books by Celeste Hamilton

Silhouette Special Edition

Torn Asunder #418
Silent Partner #447
A Fine Spring Rain #503
Face Value #532
No Place To Hide #620
Don't Look Back #690
Baby, It's You #708
Single Father #738
Father Figure #779
Child of Dreams #827
Sally Jane Got Married #865
Which Way Is Home? #897
A Family Home #938
The Daddy Quest #994
Marry Me in Amarillo #1091
Honeymoon Ranch #1158
A Father for Her Baby #1237
Her Wildest Wedding Dreams #1319

Silhouette Desire

*The Diamond's Sparkle #537
*Ruby Fire #549
*The Hidden Pearl #561

Silhouette Books
Montana Mavericks
Man without a Past

Silhouette Yours Truly

When Mac Met Hailey

*Aunt Eugenia's Treasures trilogy

Dear Reader,

In the creation of romantic heroes, some writers specialize in men whose heroic acts are spectacular rescues or daring deeds. I usually create men whose heroism comes from meeting the challenges of daily life.

My admiration for such men comes from my father, who built a strong marriage and family with my mother. The financial strains and emotional challenges of raising four children were immense. But while men all around him were leaving their families, my father held on. In my eyes, he is a true hero.

I drew on my father's strengths when I wrote
A Fine Spring Rain. Sam Bartholomew is a hardworking farmer. Left alone after his wife's tragic death, he picked himself up and went about the business of raising his children. It was a pleasure to create the perfect woman for Sam—sensitive and kind Dr. Merry Conrad. I'm proud of their story.

I'm also proud that *A Fine Spring Rain* is part of a series called AMERICAN HEROES: AGAINST ALL ODDS. To me, real heroes are ordinary people leading lives of dignity and purpose.

Sincerely,

Celeste Hamilton

Please address questions and book requests to:
Silhouette Reader Service
U.S.: 3010 Walden Ave., P.O. Box 1325, Buffalo, NY 14269
Canadian: P.O. Box 609, Fort Erie, Ont. L2A 5X3

Chapter One

The swinging doors were gun-metal gray. They were heavy. So heavy that the strain of pushing them open sent pain singing along Merry Conrad's tense muscles. Would the other side be worth the effort? No. Only more grayness—gray walls, gray floor, a long gray hall. Slowly, feeling exhaustion in every part of her body, she started walking.

Around corners, up and down stairs and through numerous sets of swinging doors she went, gathering speed. Her chest constricted in a painful knot. Her breath came in hard rasps, like an untrained bow moving across a violin's tightened strings. She could hear the switchboard paging her. She could feel the stares of the people she pushed past. But she couldn't stop. She could see that *he* was waiting, so she began to run.

He sat at the end of the hall, on a bench that looked like a narrow church pew. Not very comfortable, Merry thought, wondering why they always made people wait on hard, cramped seats. He stood as she approached. For the first time she saw the puddle of rainwater that had collected at his feet.

"They should mop that up before somebody slips and falls," she told a passing figure. But nobody listened, and she had to look back at *him*.

His eyes disturbed Merry. They were big and blue and oddly out of proportion to the rest of his face. They're just like Aunt Eda Rue's treasured china plate, Merry thought— the one on the piano back home, the plate no one was supposed to touch. His eyes were too big, too trusting, too full of hope, impossible to resist. Merry backed away.

"I'm sorry..." she began, wondering why her voice sounded so high and childish.

And like the fragile china, his blue eyes shattered, hitting the puddle of rainwater with definite little splashes....

The sound jarred Merry awake, and it took her several moments to realize the moisture on her forehead was per-spiration and not splatters of rain. She lay in the darkness and waited for the thumping of her heart to still before she sat up and switched on the bedside lamp. A reassuring pool of light washed over her familiar bedroom furniture. Swing-ing her feet to the floor, she ran a hand through her short curls and took a deep breath.

The dream was back. It was slightly different from the last time, of course. For the six years she'd been having the nightmare, each occurrence had carried with it some subtle change. Only one thing ever remained the same— the way the man's blue eyes shattered. Who says you don't dream in color? Merry thought, shuddering at the memory.

For almost five months the dream had been absent. Though she'd been worried about changing jobs and mov-ing, her sleep had been undisturbed. Stress and worry had usually caused the dream in the past, so she'd mistakenly assumed she'd conquered it. However, it had returned with a vengeance, and she knew why. It was her first night back in Bingham, Indiana—the scene of the crime.

"But it wasn't a crime," she whispered. She jumped as a tree limb scraped against the house just outside the open window.

Merry got up and closed the window. She knew she was shivering more from the dream than the late September air, but the movement was a distraction, aimed at putting the disturbing sleep-induced images from her mind. For the same reason, she took a pencil and paper from her handbag and wrote a reminder to her new landlord about trimming the tree branches away from the house. And after all this, when the shattered blue eyes still seemed frighteningly real, she slipped into her robe and stole downstairs to fix some herbal tea.

The small kitchen was a maze of half-emptied boxes, but Merry managed to find what she needed. Only when she sat at the table, her hands cupping a warm mug, did the panic begin to subside. Only then could she chide herself for letting the dream upset her.

She knew why the nightmare had started in the first place. The psychologist she'd talked with had explained that many successful people dreamed about their failures. Merry had smiled then, thinking that accountants must have columns of unbalanced figures dancing through their nightmares. She smiled now, thinking the same thing.

"I should have been an accountant," she murmured, and sipped her tea.

But she was a doctor. She could not imagine being anything else. From the moment she'd bandaged the broken arms of baby dolls in Aunt Eda Rue's basement, Merry had been sure of her calling. That confidence had sustained her through school and training, when she'd worried as much about paying the tuition as passing the tests. That confidence had brought her to her first job at the regional hospital here in Bingham six years ago.

And after leaving here everything had started to go wrong, Merry thought. Her job. Her marriage. All so wrong.

She closed her eyes and held the mug of tea to her cheek. She didn't know why so many of her choices had turned out to be mistakes. Just as she didn't understand why she couldn't shake the dream of the man with the shattered blue eyes.

He was not merely a creature of her dreams. He was a real person. Sam Bartholomew. His name, like the rain-washed smell of that spring night six years ago, was forever imprinted on Merry's brain.

It wasn't that she'd dwelt on what happened. She'd gone on with her life and her career. Not long after that spring night, she'd accepted a lucrative position with a prestigious obstetrics/gynecology clinic in Chicago. She'd met and married Colin. For a time she'd been happy. The fact that her job had become a hopeless jumble of red tape and her marriage had ended so bitterly had nothing to do with Sam Bartholomew. Just as the dream had nothing to do with her return to Bingham. Merry had accepted her new job as head of a new regional women's clinic and had come back to this small town in hopes of finding a simpler, happier life.

No, Merry hadn't let herself become obsessed with the loss of one patient, but throughout the years, usually after this dream, she found herself wondering what had happened to Sam Bartholomew. She liked to think there'd been a happy ending for him eventually; that if by chance they should meet…

Setting down her mug, Merry reminded herself where she was. There was every reason to think she might run into Sam Bartholomew if he still lived in the area. In fact, Merry decided as she pushed away from the table, she might not even have to leave it up to chance. When she got a phone book, she could look him up, give him a call.

Maybe seeing him would finally set her dreams and her mind to rest.

That seemed like a good plan in the silence of the strange kitchen in the wee hours of the morning. But the next day Merry wasn't sure. She had decided to forget it by the time she picked up her phone book at the telephone company that afternoon.

She made it all the way to her car before she tore open the book and looked up his name.

The sky was the deep blue of autumn. Against it, on the trees that lined the fence row, the occasional crimson leaf was a vivid contrast. Sam Bartholomew paused in the open doorway of the barn to admire the effect. It seemed only yesterday that he'd stopped in this exact spot to note the green growth of spring on those very same trees. Summer had slipped away from him, unnoticed.

No, not unnoticed, he corrected himself. He'd felt summer's heat, tasted summer in the salt of his own sweat, smelled it in the pungent odor of fertilizer, and heard it in the steady drone of the equipment that tended his cornfields. But he hadn't really *seen* the summer. He hadn't paused to enjoy the budding beauty of the countryside. For that Sam felt a momentary, sharp regret.

Now it would start all over again. Now he would paint the barns, work on the machinery, tend the livestock and spend the winter preparing for spring. Then, like as not, another summer would slip away. Again and again, over and over, the cycle would wind, just as it had for his father and his grandfather.

Shaking off the touch of sadness, Sam left the barn and strode across the sun-dappled yard toward the house. It was a blocklike structure, two stories high with a roof that sloped sharply in the back across a screened-in porch. Two decades older than Sam's thirty-two years, the house was showing its age in the sagging shutters and the patchwork shingles. White paint was peeling on the north side, but he resisted the urge to do something about it today. That could wait for tomorrow.

This afternoon he would give himself that well-deserved pause he'd been thinking about. The harvest was virtually over. The books were balancing in the black, if only just barely. He could rest. Since it was almost time for the school bus to deposit the kids at the end of the driveway, he decided to walk out and meet them. Rounding the front corner of the house, he halted at the sight of an unfamiliar gray car parked in front.

"Hello," called the woman who leaned against the car. "I didn't think anyone was home."

Her voice had a pleasant lilt to it, and there was something even more pleasing about the graceful way her figure moved across the yard. She was tall and slender, dressed in khaki pants and a plaid blouse with a rust-colored sweater tied loosely about her shoulders. Her short hair reflected the sun's fire in its auburn curls. By contrast her skin was pale. And she seemed familiar to Sam. He was sure no one he knew drove a car like that, but somehow she was—

Dr. Conrad. As quick as a spark from a fire her name came to Sam, and the recognition stung. This was the doctor who had told him Liza was dead. The six years between then and now collapsed quickly, and once again Sam was sitting in a waiting room, watching her walk toward him, feeling the panic hit before she said even the first grim word....

"Mr. Bartholomew?"

He blinked and reminded himself that this pain was long gone. He was standing in his own yard, and the woman who stood in front of him didn't have any bad news to impart. "You're Dr. Conrad," he said.

"Why yes, I am," Merry answered, faintly surprised that

he had recognized her. She felt as if she'd changed a great deal since that damp April night six years ago.

"How are you?"

His words were faultlessly polite, and Merry wondered at his composure even as she muttered an equally inane response. "I'm fine. And you?"

"Fine."

His eyes really are just like in my dream, Merry thought to herself—a fathomless blue. But they were the only feature she'd correctly reconstructed. She hadn't remembered the chestnut hair that curled over his forehead, the long, lean lines of his face or the muscled build.

"Was there something you wanted?"

Merry's gaze jerked up to meet his. Of course he was wondering what she was doing here. And now, facing him, her reasons seemed very silly. She couldn't, however, stop now. "I've moved back to Bingham," she began lamely.

One dark eyebrow cocked over a blue eye. "Oh?"

Stupid, Merry called herself, *he probably never knew you left.* She stumbled on. "Yes, I'm going to be in charge of the new women's clinic...and...well...I happened to think of you...of your wife...and I just wondered how you were." She was stuttering like an idiot and feeling even worse. This surprise visit had been a big mistake. She should have waited until she could reach him by telephone. But when she had called from a phone booth there'd been no answer. So she'd stopped at a gas station and asked directions to the address listed beside his number. She'd felt very brave and very sure of herself in the car. All that bravado had now deserted her.

Sam studied the woman's face in silence, wondering about her real reason for being here. Was there something about Liza's death he hadn't been told? "Is there a problem?" He took a step toward her.

Merry edged back. "No, of course not, nothing's wrong."

His eyes narrowed, betraying his skepticism. "You're sure?"

"Of course I'm sure," she answered evenly. It was a pity she hadn't foreseen how awkward this would be. But no, she had just barreled out here. Aunt Eda Rue had always cautioned Merry about her impetuous nature. As she had so many times before, Merry wished she had listened to the older woman's advice. But she hadn't, so the only thing left to do was make the best of a bad situation. That meant getting out of here as fast as she could.

Merry ran a damp palm down the side of her slacks and attempted an apologetic smile. "Mr. Bartholomew, I'm very sorry that I've intruded this way. I didn't intend to make you uncomfortable. I'll just be on my way." She turned toward her car.

"Wait a minute."

His quiet words halted her in mid-stride, and she glanced back at him over her shoulder. His tightly drawn expression and the glitter of his blue eyes sent a flicker of fear down Merry's spine. All at once she realized how vulnerable she'd made herself by coming unannounced to a strange place to confront a strange man about something that would almost certainly dredge up strong emotions. Watching him closely, she backed toward her car. He followed her.

"You must have had a good reason," he said mildly.

"A good reason?" Her words stuck like cotton in her throat.

"For coming here," he continued in the same reasonable tone. "I don't think doctors make a habit of this sort of thing, do they?"

Merry halted her retreat. He didn't sound angry, and now that he was closer she could see he wasn't really frowning, just squinting into the sun. Relief replaced her illogical fear. She realized she owed him an explanation.

"I mean, I'm not up on all medical procedures," he continued before she could speak, "but something tells me that visiting the families of the deceased this long after the death isn't exactly the norm.''

He's very calm about the whole thing, Merry marveled, drawing a deep breath. "No, this isn't normal, but I wanted to talk to you."

Hooking his thumbs into the belt loops of his worn jeans, he rocked forward a little and jerked his head back toward the house. "You want to come in?"

"No," Merry murmured. Then, for the first time, she noticed the dark bands of perspiration under the arms of his blue work shirt and the streaks of dirt on his jeans. He'd probably been out working all day and would like to go wash up and sit down. Hastily she amended, "But if you'd rather go inside we can—"

"I'm fine right here."

"Then I won't keep you long." Merry found her gaze dropping under the intensity of his. She looked beyond him, to the flat fields that surrounded the house. "I feel a little silly about coming out here now, Mr. Bartholomew, but... you see." She floundered, searching for a way to begin. "I was very young when your wife died."

"So was she."

His comment was delivered quietly, but its impact brought Merry's eyes back to his. "I know that," she murmured. "That's why it was so hard for me. It seemed so unfair. I felt so awful."

Her agitation surprised Sam. On the night Liza died this doctor had been sympathetic but rather distant and very professional. Why the concern now? "It wasn't your fault," he said.

She nodded in agreement. "I know that. There was a weakness in a blood vessel in her brain, and under the strain of labor it snapped. She was probably born with that weakness."

"I know all that." Sam's mouth tightened. He'd long

ago accepted all the reasons why Liza had died, but he didn't enjoy rehashing them.

"Yes, of course you do," Merry whispered.

Sam stared at her, noticing the way she chewed at her bottom lip as if she were wrestling with a difficult problem. Gently he prodded her on. "What is it that you want to say, Dr. Conrad?"

Her words came out in a rush. "It's just that I'd never lost a mother before that night. I'd delivered hundreds of babies by then, but I wasn't prepared for her to die—"

"Are you ever prepared for that?"

She shook her head and looked down at the ground. "Of course not, but that night..." Her eyes lifted to his again, and her voice became stronger. "I mean I wasn't even her regular doctor, I was filling in for Dr. Hughes, and I... well..." Merry gulped. "Telling you that she was dead was the hardest thing I had ever faced as a doctor."

"But you handled it."

"Of course I handled it. That's what doctors do," she replied impatiently. "But it was hard, and ever since I've wondered what you did, how you coped with everything."

"You mean the baby." He smiled, and the sudden transformation was unexpected, not only because it betrayed his lack of bitterness but because it was such a perfect smile—a flash of white that crinkled his eyes and relaxed the angular lines of his face. Merry found herself smiling back.

Sam decided the doctor's smile hadn't quite chased the troubled clouds out of her brown eyes.

"I just coped," he said simply, not knowing how else to describe the hell he'd gone through after Liza's death. "My wife was gone, but my daughter was alive, very much alive. So was my son. I had other responsibilities. I went on."

"Just like that?"

He shrugged. "What else is there to do, Dr. Conrad?"

Suddenly solemn, she gazed at him in silence for a moment. "You're right, of course, what else is there to do?"

He didn't attempt an unnecessary response, and an awkwardness settled between them.

"Well," Merry said, her voice sounding overly bright, even to her own ears. "I'm glad you're doing so well, Mr. Bartholomew."

Sam followed her around the car and opened the door. She still looked so sad that he cast about for some words of comfort. "I'm glad you came out here, Dr. Conrad."

Merry sent him a surprised glance. "You are?"

"It's pretty plain that what happened with Liza has been bothering you for a long time. I hope you've set your mind to rest."

"I hope I have, too," she replied, touched by his show of concern.

He paused and turned his head toward the main road, and Merry found her attention caught by the hand he rested on the open car door. It wasn't a particularly big hand, but the fingers were blunt-edged and strong-looking. Right now they were streaked with what appeared to be motor oil. It was a workman's hand, a sturdy tool for a practical man. The sort of man who takes the bad with the good and just keeps on going, Merry thought, admiration sweeping through her.

"There's one thing you didn't ask me about," he said, forcing her to look back up into his face.

"What was that?"

"How my daughter is doing."

"She's okay, isn't she?" Merry asked, fighting down a trace of panic. The baby she'd delivered that awful spring night had been beautiful, alert and completely normal in every respect. Surely nothing had happened later.

Again that perfect smile split Sam Bartholomew's face. "She's fine. See for yourself." He nodded toward the long, graveled drive.

Merry twisted around in her seat just as the high, sparkling laughter of children spilled through the air. From her car she watched a boy and girl race up the drive, churning dust in the wake of their flying heels. The girl was tiny, and it was obvious that she was running with all her might while her older brother merely jogged by her side. He taunted her about being slow. She yelled right back. Merry couldn't help but smile.

Their father met them in the middle of the yard, ruffled the boy's brown hair and swung the girl up in the air. She giggled with delight, and that irresistible sound drew Merry out of her car toward them.

"Who's that?" the girl asked her father as Merry approached.

With his work-stained hand, Sam brushed at the fine tendrils of chestnut hair that had escaped the bonds of his daughter's ponytail. "This lady," he said, nodding toward Merry, "is Dr. Conrad, the doctor who helped you get born."

The child's eyes were already big and blue, but Merry was sure they stretched to twice their normal size. They were a calmer, sweeter version of the eyes from her dream—her father's eyes.

"You're kiddin'," the little girl accused.

"No, I'm not."

"Did you help me, too?" the boy asked. He looked to be two or three years older than his sister, and from his tone it was obvious that he was not about to be left out of the conversation. Merry smiled down into his wide, brown eyes.

"Sorry," she said. "I wasn't around for your birthday."

"Oh," he murmured, clearly disappointed.

The glance his sister sent his way was faintly triumphant. "My name's Sarah," she told Merry.

"Yes, and this is Jared," their father said, nodding at his son.

"Tell me what I looked like bein' born," Sarah demanded.

Her father shook his head. "Sarah, don't be rude."

"Please," she added hopefully, blue eyes sparkling.

Merry wondered how anyone could deny this child anything when she turned on the charm of those eyes. She grinned as she answered the blunt question. "You were very small, and you had lots of brown curly hair."

The girl's brows drew together in a tiny frown. "How small?"

"Oh, about this big." Merry held up her hands to demonstrate.

"See, you've always been a peewee," Jared scoffed.

"Have not!" Sarah returned, trying to wiggle out of her father's arms.

"That's enough," Sam ordered, even though he let Sarah slide to the ground. Jared looked set to flee if she tried an attack.

Sarah, however, was far more interested in Merry. Her gaze was intensely serious as she asked, "So did you know my Mommy?"

Merry didn't answer immediately. Instead, she looked to Sarah's father for assistance. He didn't say a word, and his eyes were as serious as the child's. *Don't blow this one,* Merry told herself, even as she knelt in front of the child. "I only met your Mommy on the night you were born, but I remember that she was really pretty and really excited about you."

Sam didn't realize he'd been holding his breath until after the doctor had spoken. He'd always been so careful about what he said to Sarah about her mother. Never, not by any word, did he ever want his daughter to think she was to blame for Liza's death.

The answer evidently passed muster with Sarah for she smiled again. "Daddy says I look like Mommy."

"He does?" Merry murmured, glancing up at Sarah's

father. To her, the child looked more like him. But a person who had really known Liza Bartholomew might see the resemblance in a smile or an expression. Merry couldn't dispute something she knew little about, so she got to her feet and grinned down at the girl. "Well, you're awfully pretty."

"So are you," Sarah commented. "I didn't know doctors could be pretty."

"Oh, don't be dumb," Jared told her.

"I'm not!"

"Kids—" Sam interrupted the brewing argument "—why don't you go inside and get some of those cookies Aunt Beth made yesterday?"

"All right!" Jared needed no further encouragement before he bolted across the yard. An attack of manners hit him just as he reached the corner, and he called back to Merry, "Nice to meet you!" before he disappeared.

Sarah, however, lingered. "You could come, too," she said. The hand she slipped into Merry's was small and moist and sticky in the way most children's hands are.

Merry melted. She'd always been a sucker for kids, so much so that she'd been afraid to specialize in pediatrics. She'd known she would wind up too involved with her patients. So she'd contented herself with obstetrics, and in her old office in Chicago she'd kept a bulletin board filled with pictures of her latest deliveries. Nothing made her happier than seeing how much one of "her" babies had grown. Sarah deserved a very special place in that category, considering the haunting tragedy of her mother's death.

It was on the tip of Merry's tongue to accept Sarah's invitation when she happened to catch the frown on Sam Bartholomew's face. He didn't want her to stay. There were a hundred reasons why he was right. The fact that they'd shared a brief moment of loss six years ago didn't give her the right to barge into his life. Her presence was probably an unwelcome reminder of a time he had managed to put behind him. She couldn't stay.

Squeezing Sarah's hand, Merry said, "I'd love some of those cookies, but I really need to go home."

The child's bottom lip puckered just a bit. "It won't take long."

Her father stepped forward. "Sarah, if Dr. Conrad says she can't stay, she means it. Don't sulk."

Sarah's petulance disappeared instantly as a new idea seemed to take hold. "I know. You could come back Sunday and go on our picnic with us." The colored rubber band, which held her ponytail, lost its last precarious grip as the child bounced up and down with excitement.

"Sarah," Sam said in warning.

"You promised me I could ask anyone I wanted because Jared got to ask someone last time. And I want her." Sarah dropped Merry's hand and stood in front of her father, big eyes pleading. "Please, Daddy," she wheedled.

"Sarah, I'm sure Dr. Conrad has other things to do."

Since it was obvious the child's father didn't want her here, Merry knew she should turn Sarah's invitation down. But she didn't want to. After the craziness of her life over the past few years, she could think of nothing more soothing than an autumn afternoon with this enchanting little girl.

"I'd love to come," she told Sarah. "What time?"

"After church, of course," Sarah said, dancing a little jig of happiness. "I've got to go tell Jared!"

Merry laughed as the small girl darted around the corner of the house. Sarah's father was not laughing.

Guilt quickly replaced Merry's pleasure. "If you'd rather I didn't come, I'll call her with an excuse."

He shook his head.

"I just couldn't seem to say no."

The barest trace of a smile curled his lips. "That's Sarah's most obvious talent—she never lets you say no."

"She's beautiful." Merry sent a wistful glance in the direction the girl had disappeared.

"I'm glad you approve." Sam could tell by the way the doctor's mouth tightened that she hadn't missed the sarcasm in his tone. Why was this woman so interested in his family?

"I should be going," she murmured, heading toward her car. "I'll be here Sunday around twelve-thirty. What can I bring?"

"Nothing," he said, falling into step beside her.

Merry nodded, but already she was trying to think of some treat she could bring that Sarah and Jared would love. Her hand reached for the car-door handle, but Sam Bartholomew's was quicker. With old-fashioned courtesy, he stood by while she got in, and then he closed the door, giving it a little pull to make sure it was securely fastened. The gesture seemed automatic, and Merry had to smile. Most strangers didn't act so concerned about your safety.

"Mr. Bartholomew—"

"I think you can call me Sam." He stooped down a little to peer in the open window. "After all, we're not exactly strangers."

And I was just thinking we were, Merry thought. On impulse, she stuck out her hand. "Thank you for talking with me. Some people would think I was crazy or something."

Sam looked down at the proffered hand for a moment before enclosing it in his. "For all I know you could be crazy."

The strength of her grip slackened. "Oh."

"But then, you also could be the sanest person I've ever met."

A dimple Sam hadn't noticed before appeared in her cheek. "I think you're trying to say that you don't know what to think of me."

His eyebrow cocked quizzically. "Can you blame me? One minute I'm walking out of my barn, and the next minute I run right into a memory. We don't usually get this much excitement in one afternoon."

Instantly she was contrite again. "I should have waited and called you. I know seeing me, recognizing me, brought back some bad memories."

"Don't worry about it," he said, finally letting go of her hand. "I don't have any memories I'm afraid of anymore."

"Then you're a lucky man," she said softly.

Sam saw the sadness steal into her eyes again, but she started the car before he could say anything more. Stepping back, he watched until the gray sedan disappeared down the driveway. When she was gone, he realized he was clenching and unclenching the hand that held hers. He could still feel the softness of her skin beneath the callused roughness of his own. He glanced down and for the first time noticed the oil stains on his skin.

"She won't come on Sunday," he muttered, closing his hand into a fist. He couldn't think of a reason why a woman that beautiful would want to spend her Sunday afternoon with him and his children.

Chapter Two

There was rain late Friday night. As she listened to the water roll off the roof, Merry stood by a window, sipped her tea and thanked the heavens for her reprieve. Surely it would be too damp for the Sunday picnic she'd decided she couldn't attend. She wouldn't have to make up an excuse.

Saturday, however, a drying wind chased the last clouds from the sky. The forecast called for clear skies on Sunday. She hadn't been saved from her foolishness after all.

She hustled around her rented house, emptying neatly packed boxes and organizing her belongings in her usual precise, orderly fashion. The house didn't have as much room as the condominium in Chicago, but Merry didn't mind. There was space for her low, comfortable couch, her stereo and her collection of Beatles albums. Above the fireplace mantel she hung the gilt-framed landscape that had held a similar position at Aunt Eda Rue's. Perfect, she decided, giving the room an approving glance.

Late Saturday morning, she met the nice young couple who lived next door. From down the street, an elderly woman came, bearing warm-from-the-oven apple tarts. It was small town and comforting, and Merry was positive she'd done the right thing by coming back to Bingham.

Here on this tree-shaded street perhaps she could forget the possession-hungry life she'd led with Colin. At the clinic she hoped to get back to the basics of medicine: healing and helping. This was her second chance.

If only she hadn't gone out to see Sam Bartholomew everything would be perfect.

Reason had returned to her on the drive home from his farm. What she'd done was crazy, almost unprofessional. She couldn't return for a picnic the man quite clearly didn't want her to attend. Yet every time Merry thought of picking up the phone and offering an excuse for not going on Sunday, she remembered Sarah's blue, trusting eyes. In those eyes was all the hope Merry had ever lost. She had promised the child she would come. And Merry didn't break promises. Especially not to little girls who were, as she had been, motherless.

Only my mother didn't just die. She walked away from me.

That thought left its usual bitter taste in Merry's mouth. She wondered, as always, if she'd ever escape all those painful childhood memories. Sam Bartholomew may have made peace with his past, but for her it still lingered, still hurt.

He's a strong man, Merry thought. Only strong people, people at peace with themselves, could walk such an unwavering line toward the future. As she'd told him yesterday, she envied him. And the strength of that envy was matched by her desire to see him again.

"And that is crazy," she murmured. Apart from the obvious facts, she knew almost nothing about the man. For that matter, why should she want to know more? The whole idea had been to look him up just to see how he was doing. And he was fine. His child was fine. What else did she need to know? Why in the world did she have this overwhelming wish to see him, talk to him once more?

Illogically the only answer that came to mind was his dazzling, perfect smile.

She wanted to see his smile again.

And his smile, Merry assured herself, was the worst possible reason for going on the picnic. However, she couldn't talk herself into staying home. "I'll go tomorrow and that will be the end of it," she told herself late Saturday night.

So it was that Merry rose early Sunday morning and baked a pan of double-fudge brownies. For good measure, she topped them with an entire can of chocolate frosting. As she drove out to the farm, she blamed the unsettled feel of her stomach on the inordinate amount of taste-testing her baking had demanded.

Sam stood in the side yard with his cousin, Bill Kane, and watched Merry's gray sedan follow the drive to the back of his house.

Bill let out a low whistle as the car came to a halt. "Isn't that a Mercedes?"

"Looks like it to me," Sam answered tightly. He hadn't thought Dr. Conrad would show. Having decided she couldn't really be interested in picnics, he had dismissed her from his thoughts. No, he amended, he had thought about her. Who wouldn't think about a woman who barged into your life the way she had? He just hadn't expected to see her today.

Forcing a welcoming smile, he stepped forward as she got out of her car.

As expected, Merry thought, his smile was flawless. *I could go home now.* But instead she managed a "Hi, Sam," as he took the box of brownies from her. She was surprised to find her eyes almost level with his. Their other meetings had left her with the impression he was a much bigger man, but now she could see he was no more than two or three inches taller than her five foot seven. Perhaps it was his solid build that had deceived her. Quickly he introduced her to the thin, blond man who waited in the yard.

"Please call me Merry," she said, and the dimple showed in her cheek. "As in Christmas."

Merry Conrad extended her hand to Bill, and Sam was tempted to tell his cousin to put his eyes back in their sockets. Not that she wasn't an eye-popping sight. Her tight jeans outlined lean but shapely legs and hips, and her simple yellow shirt enhanced the slender but undoubtedly feminine curves of her body. Sam had never been the kind of man who paid much attention to women's clothes or jewelry but he knew what he liked. And he definitely approved of Dr. Merry Conrad's looks, from the leather ankle-high boots on her feet to the tiny gold hoops that glistened at her ears.

"Are you going on the picnic, too?" Merry asked Bill. She hoped so. If there were plenty of people around perhaps she wouldn't feel so awkward.

But Bill shook his head. "No, we just brought the kids home from church, and—"

A woman's voice cut him short, calling from the house. "Sam!"

"We're out here," Bill answered, not giving Sam a chance.

The back door opened, and Merry watched a young woman emerge from the house. Short and slim, she wore a simple blue dress, and her dark hair just brushed her shoulders. Her attention was still caught by something inside the house even as she started down the narrow, concrete steps. "Sam, do you know where Sarah's tennis shoes are? That child is so excited she would barely sit still for me to get her Sunday dress off—" At that moment she glanced toward the group in the yard and paused on the bottom step. Behind her, the screen door banged shut.

Sam swallowed, wondering why he felt so nervous. "Beth, come on out. This is Dr. Merry Conrad. She's going on our picnic with us."

This is Sam's wife, Merry thought dully. He had remarried. There had been no reason for him to mention it yesterday, just as there was no reason for her to feel this unreasonable disappointment. She didn't think he wore a wedding ring, but that didn't mean anything. Her ex-husband had rarely worn his either, although Merry doubted Sam left his off for the same reason Colin had.

"This is my sister-in-law, Beth Kane," Sam said, slicing neatly through Merry's erroneous assumptions.

"Your sister-in-law?" Automatically Merry put out her hand and smiled as she digested this new information. The other woman touched Merry's hand briefly but didn't smile.

Bill slipped his arm around the woman's shoulders. "And my wife," he said proudly.

Sam could see that Merry was having some trouble understanding the family relationships. "Beth is Liza's sister. She married my cousin Bill. We all grew up together."

"I guess it is kind of confusing to an outsider," Beth said, still not smiling as she looked at Merry. "Are you new in town?"

Merry gave a brief explanation of how she'd once worked in Bingham and had returned. "I think it's a charming place."

Beth finally gave a tight little grin, but her next question was blunt. "How is it you and Sam know each other, Dr. Conrad?"

Murmuring that Beth should use her first name, Merry tossed Sam an uncertain look. She didn't want to explain exactly who she was. Surely he didn't want her to, either. But though she waited, he gave her no assistance. Before the pause could become awkward Sarah and Jared burst out the back door.

"You really did come!" Sarah yelled, racing toward Merry.

"I said I would."

The little girl directed an accusatory look toward her father. "Daddy said you might get busy helping babies get born."

"He did?" Merry caught Sam's eye. He probably hoped I'd get busy, she thought.

"I didn't want Sarah disappointed," he explained.

"I wouldn't do that." Even as she said the words, Merry guiltily remembered praying for more rain.

Beth Kane was still after an answer for her question, and it was clear she wasn't going to be sidetracked. "Sam, how was it you said you met Dr. Conrad?"

Still Sam hesitated, and Merry bit her lip. It was Sarah who supplied the answer. "I tried to tell you about her on the way from church, Aunt Beth, but you wouldn't listen. This is the doctor that helped me be borned."

"So that's what you were jabbering about," Beth whispered, her face growing pale. "I couldn't imagine." Her husband's arm tightened around her shoulders.

Feeling the embarrassment she'd known would come, Merry drew in a deep breath.

"Isn't she pretty?" Sarah added, patting Merry's hand.

Beth nodded, obviously trying to be pleasant, even as she digested the news of Merry's exact identity.

"I thought we were goin' on a picnic," Jared grumbled. "I'm starving."

Bill's laugh sounded forced to Merry as he ruffled the boy's hair. "You're always starving, same as me." He turned to his wife. "Come on. Mother's waiting Sunday dinner for us."

Beth nodded and agreed, but her dark eyes never left Merry's face. Her words sounded clipped, as if it were all she could do to force them through her lips. "Goodbye, Dr. Conrad. I hope you enjoy the picnic." She told Jared to be good and kissed Sarah. To their father she directed only a puzzled, hurt glance.

An unhappy feeling of guilt settled in Sam's gut as he listened to Bill's old pickup crank slowly to life. He probably should have told Beth about Merry Conrad, should have known Sarah would spill the beans. But he hadn't expected the doctor to show up, and he'd obviously underestimated his daughter's continued excitement about her guest for the picnic.

He just hadn't wanted to bring up an unpleasant subject. Beth had been very close to her older sister, and to this day Sam wasn't sure she had gotten over Liza's death. His sister-in-law didn't need to be upset, especially in light of the news the couple had given him this morning. Beth was pregnant. They had wanted this baby for seven years, and Sam didn't want anything to mar their happiness.

As the pickup rattled down the drive, he glanced at Merry. Her expression was so stricken that he was instantly filled with sympathy. "Sorry about that."

"No, I'm sorry."

"About what?" Sarah piped up. Small hands braced on her blue-jeaned hips, she was frowning as she glanced from one adult to the other.

"Nothing," Sam told her.

With precocious disdain, she sniffed. "You always say that."

"I'm starving," Jared complained yet again.

Sam shook his head. No one could stay serious when his kids were around. "Then for heaven's sake get the picnic basket from the kitchen." He noticed that Merry relaxed a little.

With the basket and the box of brownies firmly in hand, they set off across the field behind the house. Merry found her unease melting under the warmth of the sun, the sight of goldenrods dancing in the breeze and the sound of Sarah's excited chatter. Jared and Sam walked ahead of them. The boy had to skip to keep up with his father's stride, and halfway across the field Merry noticed Sam had taken over the loaded basket. She watched in admiration as it swung easily at his side, obviously no burden to the work-hardened muscles of his broad shoulders.

Merry and Sarah fell behind. There was much for a little girl to discover, even along a familiar path. She paused to examine a late-blooming patch of sweet clover and then insisted on picking some for show-and-tell hour at school. An abandoned anthill had to be flattened. The putrid odor of half-dried cow dung elicited an involved but hilarious story about how Jared had fallen into a pigpen. By the time they reached the stand of trees where the other two waited, Merry was laughing so hard there were tears in her eyes.

Sam thought her the most beautiful woman he'd ever seen.

It wasn't just her delicate, even features or the rich brown of her eyes, or even her perfect figure. The core of her beauty, the most important part, was the kindness in her eyes as she talked with Sarah.

In the past few years Sam had enjoyed the company of a few women. Yet none of them had captured his interest like this woman about whom he knew so little. He wondered if his admiration made him disloyal to the memory of his wife.

Liza had been pretty, the prettiest girl in their class, so pretty that her picture in his wallet had earned him the envy of many of his friends at college. On their wedding day, as she'd walked down the aisle in her mother's ivory dress, she had glowed. But Liza's beauty had been as natural and as familiar as the gentle growth of violets against green spring grass.

Merry Conrad was altogether different, like a perfect, tissue-wrapped flower-shop rose.

At least that's what Sam thought at the beginning of the picnic. Merry soon forced him to change his mind. No hot-house flower could have so good-naturedly endured Jared and Sarah's endless squabbling, or so gamely finished a sandwich that had been knocked to the ground, or brought such enthusiasm to a stone-skipping session beside the nearby creek. She laughed often, a full, throaty sound that invariably caused everyone else to join in.

Late in the afternoon Sam sprawled back on the quilt they'd spread beneath an ancient oak and watched Merry Conrad race across the field with his children. Her hair was a tumbled mass of auburn curls and the hem of her blouse had come untucked on one side. She was obviously not fragile, despite the pale, chinalike quality of her skin. That skin was flushed now, Sam noted as she left the children and came toward him. There was straw in her hair. And she was still beautiful.

This time his reaction to that beauty was like tires squealing along asphalt. It left a path that burned all the way to his gut.

Stubbornly he refused to give in to the feeling. She might be taking a seat beside him on the blanket, and she might be as gorgeous as any model on the front of any magazine, but she was definitely not for him.

Even if I were looking for someone, she'd be off limits, Sam told himself.

"You're missing all the fun," she said as she poured some iced tea from an insulated jug.

His eyes remained on the children, who were still racing each other. "I get to have this kind of fun all the time."

"I envy you."

He cut her a skeptical, sidelong glance, thinking of the Mercedes she'd parked beside his five-year-old truck.

She continued blithely, "The picnics I went on when I was a kid were different."

There was no answering comment, but Merry kept on. "My aunt and uncle would load everything in the car, and we'd drive for what seemed like hours to find just the right picnic spot. You're very lucky—all you have to do is walk out the back door to find all this." Merry tipped her head back to admire the multicolored pattern of leaves against the clear, blue sky.

Following the direction of her gaze, Sam murmured, "I guess I take it for granted."

At last, Merry thought, she'd gotten his attention. She'd been trying to get him to talk to her all afternoon. He'd left most of the conversation to the children. "Do you and the kids come on many picnics?"

"No."

"Why?"

"There's not much time."

"With a spot this beautiful I'd probably be on a picnic every day."

"With a farm, and a house and two children, I don't have much time for picnics."

The defensive note in his voice surprised Merry. Automatically her gaze went to the space on his shirt where a button was missing. She thought of that big old farmhouse and what she'd already seen of the demands of two active children. No, she could see why he didn't have too many idle afternoons. She had to struggle to keep the sympathy she felt from showing. Somehow she knew he wouldn't take well to pity. "It's a lot of responsibility for one person."

He shrugged. "Beth gives me a hand."

"I'm sure she's a big help."

"We're family. She loves the kids."

The way he said those words, one would think families and love were naturally linked. Merry wished that were true.

Sam watched the sadness flicker across her face, just as it had the other day. What had he said that could possibly make her sad? Forgetting his resolve to maintain his distance, he sat up from his half-reclining position and cast about for some safe topic of conversation. "Where'd you grow up?"

"Lexington, Kentucky."

"Your family still there?"

"Just some cousins," Merry murmured, thinking of Jimmy and Will. Could people you barely knew really be called your family?

"Your parents?"

Her frown was a tiny line between her brows. "My parents are dead, and the aunt and uncle who raised me are gone, too."

"Oh."

He didn't push for more information as most people did. She liked that. It made her feel comfortable. She took a grateful sip of her iced tea.

"This has been such a nice day. I'm going to be thinking about it tomorrow." Merry saw the question in Sam's eyes. "It's my first day at the clinic."

"Nervous?"

"A little. But I'm excited, too. The clinic is badly needed. Too many women don't see a doctor when they need to because they can't afford it. We'll be providing care to people who might not get it elsewhere." Merry stopped, knowing that if she allowed it, she could rattle on about one of her favorite subjects all day long. Sam couldn't possibly be interested.

He surprised her by asking about the clinic's funding and staff organization. The very nature of his questions revealed the keen intelligence Merry had already suspected he possessed. She jumped at the chance to talk about her job.

Sam surprised himself by bringing the conversation back to a personal level. "Why did you come back here? Really?"

Merry faltered. His words were almost challenging. "I was tired of Chicago and my position there. This job offered everything I wanted—"

"Not money, surely. A government-funded program couldn't possibly pay as much as private practice. At least not enough to buy cars like the one you have."

Glancing away, Merry felt a flush crawl up her neck. Like most of the flashy, impractical parts of her life, the car had been Colin's idea. He had said it looked good with her hair. She'd known that was utter nonsense, but when the divorce settlement was made she'd been glad that at least the car was paid for and ran well. To her it was just transportation. Only now did she consider how pretentious it probably looked to a person such as Sam—to most of the people of this area.

Sam cleared his throat, and Merry turned back to him, wondering how she could explain herself. He spoke before she could try.

"Your car is none of my business."

"No, I don't mind," Merry protested. For some reason she wanted him to understand.

He held up a hand to silence her. "No, really. I was prying. I don't need to know why you came here. It's not important." With a swift movement he was on his feet and moving toward the field where the children still played.

Stung, Merry remained on the blanket. It was as if he had pulled a shutter down between them. One minute they had been talking, getting to know each other. Then he'd stopped it. Why? The obvious answer was the one he had given—she wasn't important. And why should she be? She was nothing to him or his children.

Draining the last of her tea, she glanced toward the field. Sam was tossing a miniature football to Jared while Sarah raced around in circles, arms extended, her piquant face turned toward the sun. It didn't matter that one member was missing, this was a family, complete unto itself. And Merry was just an outsider. Again.

She'd grown up this way—standing just at the edge. As a little girl she could remember sneaking out of bed and hiding beside the living-room door to listen to her aunt and uncle and her cousins talk and laugh. How she'd wanted to join them. Merry could still feel that empty, yearning ache in the pit of her stomach.

It hadn't been her cousins' fault. Jimmy and Will were almost teenagers when Merry was born. They treated her as kindly as they knew how, but a little girl just didn't interest them. Her aunt and uncle were kind, too. They gave her a home and clothes and cared for her when she was sick. But always, Merry knew they were watching, waiting for her to make the same mistakes her beautiful, irresponsible mother had made. Perhaps it had been because they were so busy watching that they'd forgotten to love her.

"Merry?"

Looking up, she found Sarah's big, anxious eyes on her. Only then did Merry realize she was tearing her paper cup into tiny pieces. She laid it down. "Yes, Sarah?"

The child smiled. "I want you to come and watch me be a butterfly."

"A butterfly? How?"

"Like this." Instantly Sarah was dancing through the trees, arms flapping, imagination obviously soaring.

Happiness tugged at Merry's heart as she followed the child. Today, at least, someone wanted her undivided attention, wanted her to be part of a family. That was enough to help her ignore the way Sam frowned.

Sam knew he was frowning more and more as the afternoon drew to a close. It wasn't Merry's fault. Despite the abrupt way he'd cut off their conversation, she was friendly, even charming. The frown was for himself, for the crazy, illogical way he let himself react to her. He had too much to worry about to waste thought on a fleeting attraction to an unreachable woman. He had debts to pay, land to farm, children to raise. He couldn't be sidetracked, not even for an afternoon.

He started them home when the golden autumn sunshine

began to dissolve into shadows. This time Sam carried a sleepy Sarah. Merry walked beside him while Jared scampered ahead with the nearly empty picnic basket. And Sam could think of nothing to say. Thankfully Merry didn't try to make him talk as she had earlier. She simply walked and gazed about with a thoughtful expression.

Sam tried to see their surroundings through her eyes. The flat farmland was as familiar as his own face, so he couldn't judge it. In the summer the acres were covered with green, growing corn. Now, with the harvest over, they were stripped bare, and only an occasional stand of trees broke the landscape. Did Merry find it ugly?

Certainly the farm buildings weren't a pretty sight. The three red barns and the twin silos were badly in need of paint. The dusty driveway could use a load of gravel. The grass in the yard had gone too long without mowing this summer, and against the side of the house his grandmother's treasured boxwoods had an unkempt, wild look to them. There just isn't time to do everything, Sam thought. He spared a glance for Merry's face, expecting to see distaste. She disappointed him by smiling.

He carried Sarah into the house and Merry followed, though Sam tried to think of some reason to keep her out. The big kitchen stretched the width of the house, with stove, refrigerator and cabinets in a U-shape, across one end, a long wooden table down the middle and a grouping of chairs and an old couch beside a wood stove at the other end. It was neater than usual, but with Merry in it Sam saw every nick and scratch in the table, every worn patch on the furniture. The living room at the front of the house seemed similarly shabby.

"Come upstairs and see my room," Sarah invited Merry in a sleepy voice.

Sam started to protest and held his breath as Merry hesitated. Then Sarah said, "Please," and he watched the hesitation melt. He saw cracks in the ceiling he'd never noticed before as Merry followed him up the narrow stairway.

"Are you sure you want to take a nap?" Sam asked the child as he lay her down on her bed. "It'll be bedtime before you know it."

She nodded and yawned. "I'm tired."

Merry stood in the doorway and watched the man tuck a patchwork quilt around his daughter's small form. He wore his affection for his children as naturally as most of the men Merry had known in Chicago clutched their designer briefcases. Curiously, the tenderness and patience he displayed enhanced, rather than lessened, his masculinity. Feeling like an intruder, she looked away as Sam bent to kiss his daughter.

"Do you like my room?"

It was a moment before Merry realized the child was talking to her. Quickly she said, "It's very pretty." Only then did she really glance about the small, under-the-eaves room. The rug was worn, the furniture had seen better days and toys and dolls were heaped everywhere in untidy piles. But the walls were painted a cheerful yellow with bright crayon-colored drawings to decorate them. It was a nice room. She could imagine Sarah lying on the blue gingham bedspread, listening to the rain on the roof and dreaming the usual little-girl dreams. And that, Merry knew, was the real purpose of any child's room.

A few of her own childhood dreams filled Merry's heart as her gaze locked with Sam's. Perhaps it was those dreams that made her think there was a trace of yearning in his deep, blue eyes. He blinked, and it was gone, replaced by the impersonal, cool expression he'd worn for most of the day. Merry asked herself why the disinterest of someone she barely knew could make her feel so bad.

"You'll come back, won't you, Merry?" Sarah murmured, obviously fighting sleep.

Once again Merry hesitated. Sam didn't want her back,

and she couldn't lie. "We'll ask your father," she finally said. She could feel Sam's irritation. He didn't like saying no to his daughter. She whispered a goodbye to the child and went back down to the kitchen where Jared was searching the refrigerator for a snack.

"I'm starving," he said just as Sam came into the room.

Merry opened the box she'd placed on the table. "There are plenty of brownies left."

"Aren't you taking them home?" The boy darted a quick look at his father.

"Of course not."

"Please do," Sam murmured.

"For heaven's sake, I made them for the children." Merry didn't try to keep the impatience out of her voice. The man acted as if she was offering a handout.

He nodded reluctantly. Jared thanked Merry and sat down at the table to eat.

"After you finish you can come out to the barn and help me with the milking," Sam told the boy.

Merry was surprised; she'd thought him a corn farmer. "You have a dairy, too?"

"Hardly." The edges of Sam's mouth quirked slightly. "I have a couple of cows that I milk for my own use and Beth's. She makes butter."

"Really?" Merry said, thinking that surely it would be easier to just buy such an inexpensive item.

Sam seemed to correctly read her mind. "You'll find most farmers to be pretty self-sufficient."

Merry was trying to think of a response that would cut through his smug tone when Jared interrupted. "I'm still hungry."

Without thinking, she suggested, "Why don't I put together some dinner while you two do the milking?"

"No," Sam answered quickly. He tried to take the harshness out of his words by adding, "It's really not necessary."

"But I had such a nice day, I'd like to repay you—"

"Really, you don't—"

"I'd really like to, please—"

"No!" The word was blunt, sharper than Sam had intended. Merry and his son stared at him.

"Fine," she said. "I'll be going." Her goodbye to Jared was warm, but she barely glanced at Sam as she left the kitchen and crossed the screened-in porch.

You're stupid, stupid, stupid, she told herself. *The man doesn't want you around. Accept it. Quit trying to horn in where you don't belong.* Her fingers had just touched the cool aluminum of the screen door when Sam's voice stopped her.

"Merry." It was the first time he'd used her first name.

Just let her go, a voice inside him urged. He ignored it. "I didn't mean to be rude."

She turned. "Yes you did." Even in the twilight dimness of the porch she could see he was surprised by her response. She continued, "I make you uncomfortable, which I guess is only normal, considering how it was that we first met."

"It's not that," he began and stopped guiltily. He couldn't tell her the real reason he wanted her to go and never come back. He couldn't say how attracted he was to her. She would probably laugh.

She laughed anyway, and the sound wasn't very pleasant. "Well, for whatever reason—you don't like me. Now you've been very nice—I've figured out that good manners just come naturally to you—but you really don't have to continue. In fact, I'd prefer it if you'd just be honest and tell me to go the hell home." She stopped abruptly, realizing too late that her little speech was irrational and uncalled for. Of course, those two adjectives described all her actions since she'd decided she *had* to track down Sam Bartholomew.

"All right," he said, stepping closer, so close that Merry

could feel the heat that radiated from his sturdy, masculine form. If her back hadn't already been against the door, she would have retreated. His voice dropped to a whisper. "Go home."

"And don't come back," Merry added, bringing her chin up. "Don't forget that part."

Sam nodded, but the words stuck in his throat. He was intensely aware that if he took half a step forward his body would touch hers, that if he lowered his head, his mouth would close on the sweet lips she seemed to be offering. He was tempted, oh-so-tempted to follow his reckless inclination. Acknowledging that, his heart began to pound. With each beat, he could feel the rust chipping away from a door he'd closed long ago.

Gazing into his eyes, Merry was swamped by a strong, inescapable feeling of shame. Why was she trying so hard to upset this decent, honest man? Was she hoping for some kind of forgiveness for letting his wife die? That didn't make sense since Liza's death hadn't been her fault. Perhaps she saw in his family the sort of contentment she'd hoped to find with Colin. The only thing she knew for certain was that a psychologist would have a field day with the whole situation.

Reaching behind her, still staring into his eyes, she grasped the door handle. Her gaze lowered a bit and centered on Sam's mouth, the stern mouth that seemed to frown much easier than it smiled. He moistened his lips as if he were about to speak, and Merry watched the movement with an out-of-proportion fascination. It hit her then. The reason for her ridiculous behavior had nothing to do with his wife or his family. It came down to a matter of chemistry. He was a man; she was a woman. They saw something in each other. The attraction lay between them, as real as a tug-of-war rope. And she knew if either of them pulled hard enough, the game would begin.

She was afraid. So she left.

The door slapped against the house as she took sure, steady steps away from the porch. Away from Sam. Merry started her car and turned it around so she could head down the drive. But like Lot's wife in the Biblical story, she couldn't resist looking back. The kitchen lights snapped on, and she saw Sam, still in the same spot, outlined against the screen door.

The car's tires spun in the gravel as Merry pushed hard on the accelerator, anxious to get away.

Sam watched her go, so centered on the fading red glow of the taillights that nothing registered until Jared's voice sounded from the kitchen doorway. "Dad! Telephone!"

"All right, all right." He whirled around and went inside. Jerking the receiver off the kitchen counter, he growled a hello.

"Sam? Is something wrong?" Beth's clear voice sliced through his preoccupation.

"Sorry," he muttered. "I was about to tend to the milking."

"This late?"

He hesitated, but decided to be truthful. "Mer—uh, Dr. Conrad just left."

"Oh." Beth was silent a moment. "She's the reason I called."

"I know. I should have told—"

"Sam, don't apologize. You didn't have a chance to tell me about it, what with Bill and me being gone yesterday and our springing our big news on you right after church."

"Still, I should have—"

"What was there to tell? Liza has been gone for over six years. I've got to stop going into a tailspin every time the subject of her death comes up."

"You don't do that," Sam assured her, though it was at least partially true.

"Yes, I do," Beth insisted but then changed the subject.

"Just tell me one thing. How did Dr. Conrad end up on your picnic?"

Briefly Sam outlined what had happened when Merry had stopped by the farm on Friday.

"It's kind of nice of her to be concerned after all these years, isn't it?" Beth commented.

"I suppose."

"She certainly doesn't look like your average doctor, does she?"

Sam closed his eyes, remembering every detail of exactly how Merry did look. "No, she doesn't."

"But she seemed very pleasant."

"Yes, very pleasant," Sam repeated. To himself he added, *and very desirable.*

Beth sighed. "I suppose I should apologize to her."

"No, I don't think so."

"Are you sure?" she pressed. "I was rather rude."

"Beth, I'm sure she understood. She's a very—" He drew a deep breath before continuing. "She's a very understanding woman." Now why had he said that? He didn't know if she was understanding or not.

There was silence on the other end of the phone.

"Beth?" Sam asked. "You still there?"

"Yes, I'm here. I guess I should let you tend to those cows."

"Yes. I'll see you tomorrow, right?"

"Just as usual. I'll be over to do a few things around the house."

"I want you to start taking it easy," Sam cautioned. "Whenever you don't feel like helping us out, just let me know. The important thing is this baby."

She laughed. "Don't you start treating me like an invalid. Bill's bad enough. I'll see you tomorrow."

"Okay. See you then." Sam replaced the phone in its cradle on the wall and stood for a moment with his forehead leaning lightly against the uneven planks of the paneling.

"Dad, do I still have to help with the milking? I've got homework."

Sam turned to face his son, who was eating a peanut butter and jelly sandwich even as he spread schoolbooks across the kitchen table. "You mean you didn't do it Friday? I thought—"

"Daddy, my stomach hurts." Sarah appeared in the doorway from the living room, rubbing her eyes sleepily.

"Too many brownies," Sam murmured.

"Dad, do I?" Jared demanded again.

It's back to reality, Sam decided. Chores to be done. Children to be answered. Simple tasks, far removed from beautiful women in cars with price tags that could pay his mortgage. He would forget her, forget whatever temptation she might have offered him tonight.

Only later, when the children were asleep, did he have time to feel the slightest twinge of regret.

Friday night, well after seven o'clock, Merry unlocked her kitchen door and dripped inside. Her medical bag landed on the butcher-block table, her umbrella hit the floor and her plastic raincoat followed suit. The untidiness was completely at odds with her nature, but she decided she simply didn't care.

"God, what an awful night," she announced. The only answer was the soggy squish of her shoes as she walked across the linoleum. I need a pet, she decided as she headed upstairs, something to meet me at the door every night. One of those shaggy, non-pedigreed dogs that Colin had especially hated would be just the right thing. Even the thought of that secret, belated revenge made her smile.

Merry knew she'd smiled a lot this week. In fact, she'd probably used up her allotment of happiness for the next three weeks. But she didn't care. She was incredibly glad to again be working where the main objective was medical *care*, not medical *cost*. Certainly she had a budget to attend to, but the bottom line was healing, not profit.

This had been an organizational week, a time for learning procedures and paperwork before the clinic opened on Monday. Merry had spent most of her time getting to know the young doctor, the three nurses and the office personnel who would report to her. She liked what she'd found. All of them seemed bright and dedicated.

She had immediately developed a rapport with one of the nurses, Amy Galveston, a petite brunette in her late twenties. Amy spent a lot of time moaning about being single in a town the size of Bingham, but at the same time she had a date almost every night of the week. On the one night she was free, she had shared a meal and plenty of girl talk with Merry at one of the town's two steak houses.

Merry had also seen some of the doctors she'd worked with at the regional hospital during her other, brief stay in Bingham. Several of them were volunteering their services for a few hours each week at the clinic. Included in the group was Dr. Jeff Cole, with whom Merry had stayed in touch over the years. Jeff had been the one who'd told her about the opening at the clinic. He was divorced now, and he'd taken Merry to lunch today. She'd almost told him how she'd tracked Sam down. Embarrassment had kept her mouth closed. She didn't need anyone to tell her how foolishly she had behaved.

Slipping out of her damp suit and into a warm sweater and jeans, Merry allowed herself to think about Sam. More correctly, she thought about that hot, expectant moment she'd shared with him on his back porch. If things were different, if they'd met under other circumstances, she wondered how the moment might have ended. Would she have run away? The question was tantalizing.

She was still searching for an answer half an hour later when she answered the doorbell. Perhaps it was the direction her thoughts had taken that caused a hot flush to rise in her cheeks.

For it was Sam who stood on her front porch. Sam—hair damp, wearing crisp jeans and a red sweater, whose apologetic, faintly nervous grin didn't in any way diminish his solid male vitality. Sam—who surprised her by saying, "We haven't had too much luck with rainy nights or porches. Do you think I could come in?"

Chapter Three

With a brass poker Sam pushed a log into position and watched as orange flames licked around the sides and caught hold. Merry had been building the fire when he'd appeared at her door, so he had volunteered to finish the job while she fixed some coffee. She'd been in the kitchen a long time; the fire was roaring. He wondered if he should go and see what was keeping her.

"No," he muttered, and shoved his hands deep in his jeans pockets. He couldn't just go wandering through her house. Instead, he glanced around the room. The colors were a surprise. For some reason he had expected feminine pastels, not this comfortable mix of beige, yellow and deep rust. Yet he could see that this suited her. Reflected firelight danced across a trio of gleaming copper baskets, reminding him of the sun in her auburn hair.

"Here we are."

Her voice roused him from his contemplation, and Sam watched Merry cross the room and deposit a tray on the low coffee table. Besides coffee she'd brought cheese, crackers and a plate full of cookies.

"You went to a lot of trouble," he said, taking a seat on the couch.

Merry poured the coffee. "Nonsense. I was hungry." Actually putting the tray together had given her a chance to collect her wits. Sam had been the last person she'd expected to see tonight. She handed him a steaming mug.

"Haven't you eaten dinner yet?"

"No. I worked late." She surprised him by claiming an overstuffed floor cushion for her seat. She was just across the table from him. Close enough to touch.

He leaned back, trying to relax. How was it she could look so calm when he felt as if he were on pins and needles? He had driven around the block four times before he'd gotten up enough courage to stop.

"How did you find me, anyway?" she asked.

He shrugged. "You said something about renting a house on Sycamore. I looked for your car."

"It does sort of stand out, doesn't it?" The teasing note in her voice eased Sam's tension a bit.

"I shouldn't have criticized it."

Being careful not to look at him, she selected a cracker and sliced off a hunk of cheese. He'd already said how sorry he was for the way they'd parted on Sunday. Merry felt guilty; the entire situation had been of her own making. "You've already apologized. I shouldn't have barged in on your family picnic."

He echoed her words, "You already apologized for that."

"So I guess we have no more apologies left to make."

"I guess not." Over the rim of his mug, Sam's eyes met Merry's and held, and he thought of that moment on his porch when she'd been only a breath away. For a minute the only sound in the room was the hiss and crackle of the fire.

It was only when he looked away that Merry realized she'd been holding her breath. She glanced around, searching for a safe topic and noticed the brightly colored drawing that lay on the end table. "Thank you again for bringing me Sarah's picture."

He set his mug down and picked up the picture, a fond smile curving his lips. "What she lacks in talent, she makes up for in color."

Merry cocked her head to the side and studied the picture he held up for her to see. The drawing had four orange stick people, two big and two small, and they appeared to be dancing in a meadow of purple, yellow and green flowers. Across the bottom in wobbly letters was printed Sunday. Merry grinned. "You know, Sam, I've seen paintings labeled as art that were much less interesting than this."

"Oh yeah? Maybe she'll make me rich some day." His smile broadened.

That smile, she told herself, was one that every actor in Hollywood would die for. Would a person ever grow tired of being on its receiving end? This time she looked away.

"Sarah really wanted you to have this picture," Sam said. "In fact she made me promise I'd bring it to you."

"And you don't deny her much, do you?"

"Not when she begs." Feeling dishonest, Sam laid down the picture and picked up his coffee mug. Sarah hadn't really begged him to deliver the picture. She'd merely asked him, and he had jumped at the chance to come here— to be with Merry.

How was it, he wondered, that he had managed to avoid the loneliness for nearly six years? Oh sure, right after Liza died, he'd felt pretty alone. But he'd adjusted. He'd done just fine—until this week. This week the minutes and hours had crawled by with agonizing slowness as he tortured himself with thoughts of a woman with kind brown eyes and an easy way of laughing. He had told himself to forget it. He had warned himself of trouble ahead. Yet here he was.

And now what do I do?

"Where are the kids?" Merry asked.

"Spending the night at Beth's."

"So you're at loose ends?"

"I was going to the high school football game—" Sam glanced at the rain-streaked window "—but it's rained so much they postponed it until tomorrow night."

"I've watched games in worse weather."

"You're a football fan?"

Merry laughed. "Don't look so surprised. I happen to have had Chicago Bears' season tickets for the last five years."

"You're kidding."

"No. I've sat out in rain, snow and sub-zero freezing temperatures. The only games I missed were the times I got called to the hospital to deliver a baby."

"You're going to miss it."

"Miss what? The games or being called to the hospital?"

They laughed together, and Sam realized with a start that he had relaxed, that he was actually enjoying himself. "Do you think you'll be running to the hospital as much here?"

She shook her head. "Probably not."

"Is that one of the reasons you left the city?"

Merry refilled her mug and paused for a moment to savor the rich aroma of the coffee and to consider Sam's question. He'd asked her once before why she'd come to this town. This time she was determined to give him an answer. "Living in the city is very complicated, Sam. Everything's always a rush. You hurry home, lock your door, then unlock it the next morning to scurry back to work. Life just pushes by you."

"That can happen anywhere you live."

She glanced at him in surprise. "Why do you say that?"

"Because I've done it. I get so wrapped up in my work that I don't notice what's going on around me." He stopped and looked down, but not before Merry saw the sadness in his blue eyes. He continued, "I turn around and a whole season has passed without my noticing, or I look at Jared and he's grown two or three inches since the last time I really looked at him."

Softly Merry said, "Sometimes you wonder if you're going to wake up someday and realize that you're old and that you haven't done half the things you intended to do."

Struck by her understanding, Sam looked up. "That's it. That's exactly the way I feel."

"Small town or big city, I guess people have regrets," Merry murmured. Since he seemed to be in an open mood, she decided to dig a little deeper. "What are your regrets, Sam?"

He didn't even hesitate. "That I didn't finish college."

"And why was that?"

"Dad died when I was a sophomore. I finished the year, but then I had to come home and run the farm for Mother. She wasn't in the best of health, either." Sam glanced at the fire, thinking back to that troubled time. "She hated asking me to come home."

"Then college was important to her, too?"

"Definitely."

Merry was puzzled. "From what I remember of the farm families I met when I lived here before, college wasn't exactly a priority with most of them."

Nodding, a faraway look in his eyes, Sam said, "My mother was different. She'd have gone to college herself if she could have figured out a way. She thought a person could never get too much education."

"Smart woman."

Sam looked back at Merry. "Yes, she was. Very smart. She read all the time—magazines, books, poetry. She kept the library busy. My dad said she'd send him to the poorhouse with her reading if he didn't watch it."

"So your father wasn't so set on education?"

"He thought it was fine—for some people."

"Not you?" Merry pressed.

The shake of his head was emphatic. "Not for anyone who wanted to be a farmer. He thought the best teacher for that was experience."

"I'm surprised you went at all."

"Mother made sure of it." Sam smiled ruefully. His simple statement was a mild description of the battles that had raged between his parents before he'd gone off to college.

Merry wondered at the smile. "I guess you're an only child, right?"

"No, my older brother, Mike, coaches football at a small college in New Hampshire."

"Couldn't he have come home or helped out until you finished college?"

"He had just gotten married, had his first job. I couldn't ask him to come back. The farm was to be mine anyway. He had no interest in farming."

Merry pressed on, "But still—"

"You don't understand," Sam cut in.

His curtness surprised her. "Why do you say that?"

"You just don't," he insisted, shifting uneasily on the couch. A glance around the comfortable room told him she couldn't possibly have ever worried about paying the electric bill.

His thoughts were easy to read, and it bothered Merry that he assumed all she'd achieved had come easily. Quickly she set him straight. "I went to college on a scholarship and medical school on a loan and the proceeds of a small life-insurance policy my uncle had taken out. It wasn't easy."

"But everything's worked out," Sam murmured, giving another pointed look at the wool rug on the floor, the framed paintings on the wall. "Obviously."

"Sure it has. But the most important thing is that I love what I do. Don't you?"

He blinked at her abrupt question. "Well, yes I do."

"Then maybe you don't have any regrets after all."

One of his eyebrows lifted at the challenge in her words. "Sure I do."

"Like what?"

"I regret that farming doesn't pay enough for cars like yours."

They laughed together then, and Merry's faint irritation with the assumptions he'd made about her disappeared. "I bet you'd never buy a car like that."

"You're right. I'd use the money for a new silo, college for the kids and a new roof on the house."

"Which shows you've got your feet on the ground."

Except about you, Sam thought, staring at the outline of her perfect features against the soft glow of the fire. With her, he could easily forget every practical thought he'd ever had. Recognizing that dangerous fact, he knew he should leave before he became any more fascinated.

But he stayed. He put another log on the fire. Merry made another pot of coffee. Outside, he could still hear the steady beat of the rain against the edge of the porch. Inside, there was only the sound of their voices, rising when they argued a little, dissolving into laughter often. Sam talked about things he hadn't discussed with anyone in years—his mother's lingering illness and death, his worries about the children. The people he knew didn't talk about these kind of subjects. They were concerned with local politics, the price of corn and the score of the most recent ball game. Sam realized that for him there'd been too many long hours of work followed by too many long nights with only the children for company. Feeling as if a dam had burst inside him, he talked for hours. He had only to look long enough into Merry's dark brown eyes to believe he could tell her anything.

The clock on the fireplace mantel chimed eleven and then twelve, and still Sam stayed. He didn't want to leave, not when he still hadn't discovered why a woman as beautiful and as easy to be with as Merry didn't have a husband and children of her own. It was only when she stifled a third yawn that he decided he might be outlasting his welcome.

Merry walked him to the small front foyer, and when she opened the door they both shivered in the chilly breeze. "I'm really glad you came by, Sam. Tell Sarah thank you for the picture."

"You could tell her yourself."

She hesitated, not knowing what he meant. "I'll call her."

"No... I mean yes, you can call her if you'd like, but what I was thinking was—" Sam stopped, suddenly unsure of what he was about to ask.

"Yes?" she prompted.

His words rushed out. "Why don't you come to the game with us all tomorrow night? The whole town will probably be there. Beth and Bill are coming. This team beat us by three points last year, and the players are bound to be psyched up. I know it won't be as exciting as a pro game or anything, but I think you'd enjoy it and—"

"Sam," Merry interrupted, giving him a gentle smile. "You don't have to convince me. I'd love to go. What time should I be ready?"

As they finalized the plans, Sam's pleasure was obvious, flattering Merry. He acted as if he'd expected her to turn him down. This trace of uncertainty from a man so attractive and so intelligent was to Merry a refreshing change. Her ex-husband had exuded enough smooth confidence to last the rest of her life.

She was smiling, her mind already leaping ahead to the next night as she and Sam said their final goodbyes. By the time she heard his car door slam, anticipation was pumping through her like adrenaline.

A date with Sam.

Of course, some people wouldn't call it a date since he

was bringing his children along. But for Merry it was close enough. Feeling as she hadn't since she was fifteen and had been invited to the homecoming dance, she peeked around the edge of the curtains that covered the door's glass panel. The headlights of Sam's truck came on and he pulled away from the curb. She watched until the darkness and the falling rain swallowed the last trace of him.

Humming a happy little tune, Merry went back to the living room. On the couch where Sam had sat, the overstuffed cushions still bore the imprint of his body. On impulse she sat down in that same spot and immediately imagined that the warmth of his skin still clung to the tweedy upholstery. She crossed her arms over her chest and closed her eyes, wondering what it would feel like to be held in his arms.

Saturday morning after the early chores Sam drove over to his cousin's farm to pick up the children. Last night had made him happy, so naturally he told Beth about it.

After his pronouncement he watched his sister-in-law put down the fork she'd been using to scramble eggs. Slowly she turned away from her stove and reacted to what he'd just told her. "You asked the doctor to the ball game?"

He grinned. "Her name is Merry. And yes, I asked her. Anything wrong with that?"

Beth shook her head and wiped a hand on the blue-checked apron that covered her faded jeans and flannel shirt. "No…I mean, yes…I mean, why would she want to come?"

Feeling his smile slip a little, Sam answered, "Because she likes football, I guess."

"I can't imagine." Beth gave a little cluck of disbelief as she went back to her cooking.

Sam's smile disappeared completely, and the wonderful feeling of happiness that had gripped him ever since he'd left Merry last night began to crumble. "What do you mean?'' he said to Beth's back. ''What can't you imagine?''

''She just doesn't seem like the type who would come to a high school game.'' The eggs joined several slices of bacon on a blue-rimmed plate as Beth talked. ''In fact she doesn't even look like the type who'd be living in a place like Bingham.'' She put the plate on the table in front of Sam.

He watched her take a seat across from him, and silently he accepted the cloth-wrapped basket of biscuits she offered. He'd spent many hours sitting at this kitchen table with Beth, talking about the children, sharing a good dinner with her and Bill. She'd done a lot for him, and perhaps that was why it seemed so important that she not have the wrong impression of Merry.

''She was tired of living in Chicago,'' he explained.

''And why is that?''

''She said everything moved too fast.''

''She'll probably be complaining that it moves too slow here.''

Sam stopped buttering a biscuit and looked at her. ''Passing judgment a little fast, aren't you?''

''Maybe I am.'' Beth had the grace to look a little ashamed. ''But Sam, don't you think it's awfully strange the way she just showed up here?''

''I explained that.''

''But now that she's seen you and she's seen Sarah, what else does she want?''

''It's not a question of wanting anything—'' Sam began.

''Then why did she invite you over last night?''

He paused. Where had Beth gotten that idea? ''She didn't invite me. I invited myself.''

''Oh.'' Beth's pale face colored. She looked down at her coffee cup. ''I see.''

''And what does that mean?'' Sam was beginning to feel a bit irritated with his sister-in-law's attitude.

"Sam, I just don't want you to get hurt."

His knife clattered against the plate as he stared at her. "Hurt? Why would I be hurt?"

She looked embarrassed. "Sam, if you're lonely, if you're thinking that it's time you found someone—"

"Wait a minute, slow down, will you? Who said I was trying to find someone?" He didn't even try to keep the impatience from his voice.

"Well, you're going out with this lady doctor—"

"I'm not *going out* with her," Sam muttered, mimicking Beth's tone. "I went to her house, had a little coffee and we're going to the ball game. For heaven's sake, the kids will be there."

"Would you rather I stayed home and kept them?"

"No, I would not," he returned sharply. At the startled look in Beth's brown eyes, he was instantly contrite. "I'm sorry, Beth, but I don't understand why this is such a big deal."

"That's because you're not looking beyond her pretty face."

Sam flushed and looked down at his plate. Merry's pretty face was what he'd thought about all night, that and her slow, sweet smile.

Beth's hand came across the table to cover his. "Sam, I don't want you to take what I'm going to say the wrong way. You're a good-looking man and you've always been lots of fun. But really, when you get right down to it, what do you and someone like Merry Conrad have in common?"

It was on the tip of his tongue to tell her all that he and Merry had talked about last night, all the things that had seemed so funny and so important. They'd talked about ideas, about dreams and feelings—the sort of talk he used to share with his mother and Liza. But unlike them or Merry, Beth didn't have a dreamer's soul. She saw only the here and now, the basic realities of getting through each day. She wouldn't understand. So he said nothing.

"I just don't want you to get hurt," Beth repeated. "She's a beautiful woman. She's probably very nice. But where can it lead?"

"I'm not saying it has to lead anywhere," Sam protested feebly.

Softly, and with precision, Beth asked, "Then what's the point?"

Like a crafty thief, her reasoning robbed Sam of the magic he'd carried with him since being with Merry.

And Beth's words echoed through Sam's mind for the rest of the day. He took the kids home. The rain was over, and he managed to finish painting the smaller of the two barns. By late afternoon he was tired, but wearily he scrubbed the paint off his hands and got the kids ready to go to the game.

Beth is probably right, he told himself as he drove through the fading early October twilight. He and Merry had nothing in common. His life was wrapped up in the land and his children and his home. She was a career woman. Most years he felt lucky just to pay the bills and have a little left over. Quite obviously she made plenty of money.

What could she possibly see in me? he was asking by the time he rang her doorbell. But even that negative thought couldn't kill the flash of desire he felt when she opened the door.

There was nothing spectacular about her brown corduroy jeans or her rust-colored turtleneck sweater. No, what caused him to react was just her. Just the way her eyes sparkled, the way her rosy-tinted lips spread wide in a welcoming smile.

"Hi, Sam," she said, sounding a little breathless.

"Hello, Merry." *Dammit, why couldn't he muster just a bit, a tiny bit of indifference to this woman?*

"Do you think I'll need a jacket?"

"Probably."

"Then let me get one."

As she disappeared back into the house, Sam turned and looked toward the truck. Both kids had their faces pressed to the passenger window, watching his every move. And Beth thought I was going on a date, he thought with a rueful shake of his head.

"Okay, I'm ready." Merry joined him on the front porch and shut the door behind her.

"You're sure you still want to go?" he asked as they started down the steps.

"Sure." Frowning, she scanned his face. "Is there something wrong?"

"No, of course not."

The truck door opened then, and Sarah, who obviously could stand to wait no longer, jumped to the sidewalk. "Merry, Merry, Merry," she called, running forward. "I'm so glad to see you!"

Jared's greeting was a trifle less enthused but no less genuine, and Merry found herself feeling happy enough to burst. The usual bickering of the children filled the drive to the high school, leaving Merry and Sam few opportunities to exchange a word. He kept asking the kids to quiet down. Merry was secretly glad when they didn't. They sounded like a family; they made her feel as if she belonged. She knew the emotion was borrowed, but she clung to it anyway, as hard as Sarah's little hand clung to hers.

The high school stadium was packed. Merry had forgotten the excitement that could fill the air on a high school football evening. The feeling was captured in the aroma of hot buttered popcorn and the strident catcalls of loyal fans. As the cool autumn breeze fanned over the crowd she could almost taste the anticipation. The mood matched her own.

Glancing at Sam as they threaded their way through the crowd, she wondered if he'd looked forward to tonight as much as she. Of course, her excitement was hugely out of proportion to the occasion, but that didn't stifle the thrill that chased up her spine as her gaze locked with his. Surely he could feel what vibrated between them. Surely he would acknowledge it in some way.

But a split second later he was turning away, leaving Merry with an illogical feeling of disappointment.

Bill found them soon after that and led the way up the bleachers to where Beth was holding a group of seats. The smile the woman sent Merry was almost friendly—but only almost.

"Come sit with me," Beth called to Sarah, patting the seat beside her.

The child shook her head. "No, I wanna sit with Merry."

For a moment, Beth's pretty features twisted in what Merry thought was resentment. The expression was quickly masked, however, and Merry wondered if it had been her imagination. At any rate, she arranged a compromise by seating the child between herself and Beth.

The first half of the game was a seesaw match of traded scores and quick turnovers. Under any other circumstance Sam probably could have lost himself in the contest. Instead he was intensely aware of Merry squeezed tight against his side on the crowded bleacher. She was close enough for him to catch the delicate fragrance of her perfume, to feel the tensing of her body when the home team went for the score on a fourth down. He was so wrapped up in Merry that he missed a touchdown, and she caught him staring. He flushed, and her grin told him she knew exactly what was going on.

Yet even his physical response to her nearness couldn't change Sam's mind about their chances for having any kind of relationship. In his mind last night's companionship had been explained away as a fluke. Beth's well-sown doubts had taken root, making him sharply attuned to how different Merry was from him and his family and friends. She even talked differently; her words were precisely spoken, never drawled. The set of her shoulders, the grace of her gestures, the very cut of her tan suede jacket seemed to set her apart.

At halftime, Sam stood up to get everyone some hot chocolate. It was an excuse, really, to put some distance between him and Merry. A tap on his shoulder stopped him.

"Hello, Sam."

He turned to find Joe Davidson, a fellow he knew from high school, standing beside him on the concrete stairs.

Sam and the burly six-footer had never been exactly friends, but still he smiled easily and greeted him. "Hi, Joe, how're you doing?"

"Obviously not as well as you." The man's eyes rested speculatively on Merry, who was busy explaining something to Sarah.

Knowing the man wouldn't rest until he'd been introduced, Sam got Merry's attention and did the honors.

They exchanged pleasantries for a moment, and then the men moved off down the steps toward the concession stands.

"Playing in the majors with that one, aren't you?" Joe asked. He disappeared into the crowd before Sam could come up with a suitable response.

He got the hot chocolate and returned to the stands, but for the rest of halftime he was busy introducing Merry. Neighbors and friends kept stopping by his seat and looking at her with questioning eyes. Everyone was friendly—on the surface. But Sam wondered what was going on in their heads. Were they, as he suspected, laughing at the preposterous sight of good old Sam Bartholomew with someone as beautiful, as out of his league as Merry?

The game didn't end any too soon for him.

Jared begged to spend another night with his aunt and uncle, but Sarah wanted to be where Merry was. That was fine with Sam since he didn't want to be alone with Merry. Of course, Sarah fell asleep in the car so her presence didn't really help after all.

Merry tried several times to start a conversation, but Sam's responses were curt dead-ends. She gave up finally and simply stroked Sarah's hair and enjoyed the feel of the warm little body that rested so trustingly against her own.

They left the child curled on the seat, a blanket tucked around her, while Sam escorted Merry to her front door. She'd left the light burning on the porch, so it was easy for Sam to see the puzzled look in her brown eyes.

"Did I do something wrong?" she asked.

"Of course not."

"Well, you've acted like you were upset about something all night long."

"Have I?"

Merry gave him a long, measured look. Perhaps it had been her imagination. By nature he seemed to be a quiet man. The amount of talking he'd done last night was probably unusual. "At any rate, I enjoyed the game. Thank you for taking me."

"Sure." With a rather abrupt movement, Sam started to leave. "Good night."

"Sam—"

He turned back to her, but he seemed impatient. "Yes?"

Feeling nervous, she cleared her throat. "Maybe you and the kids could come for dinner tomorrow night. I could cook up a big pot of chili and—"

"I don't think so."

She pressed on. "If you have other plans we could do it some other night, even next weekend if you want. I—"

"No." In his voice there was the unmistakable ring of finality.

But Merry had never been one to give up something she wanted without a fight. And she wanted to spend more time with this man. Soon. "Can I ask you why?"

Sam didn't answer right away. It would be easier to give in; he wanted to give in. But as Beth had said this morning, what would be the point? Inevitably Merry would become bored, would realize they had nothing in common. Then there would be pain and eventually bitterness. He'd had more than his share of both those emotions. It was better to walk away now.

"I don't think we should spend any more time together," he said bluntly.

Her eyes grew round with hurt and surprise. "I don't understand."

A cool gust of wind blew across the porch, rattling the drying leaves that had collected in the corners. Merry shivered, and on reflex Sam reached out and pulled the two sides of her jacket together. Automatically it seemed, his hand moved upward until his knuckles lightly grazed the smooth line of her jaw. He closed his eyes, thinking it a shame that he would never touch her skin again. Her hand closed over his, holding it against her cheek.

"I don't understand," she whispered again, stepping forward.

Before Sam could open his eyes or realize her intent, her mouth was against his.

It could have been an innocent kiss, especially if Sam had used his head and backed away. But he didn't. Instead, the hand that cupped her face fanned through the short, wispy curls of her hair and urged her ever closer to the questing pressure of his lips. Desire spread like an ache to every part of his body.

Now it will be hard to forget, he thought, even as they continued to kiss; now that I know the taste of her lips, I'll have one too many things to regret.

With reluctance, he drew away. Intentionally he avoided looking into her eyes. He knew they would be wide, and dark and velvety with passion. He couldn't risk seeing that look. Instead, he turned on his heel and walked purposefully down the walk to the truck where his daughter lay sleeping.

Tonight Merry didn't watch him leave. Hurriedly she

unlocked the door and went into her snug, warm little house. She turned on the radio—loud—hoping it would drown out the sound of his truck pulling away.

It won't happen again, she thought.

All her life people had been leaving her. Her mother had left physically. Aunt Eda Rue and Colin had withdrawn from her in spirit. And now this. Merry had gotten just a glimpse of something she thought could make her happy— an honest, sweet man with a family to match. She didn't know what had happened between last night and now to make Sam pull away, but he'd slammed the door in her face.

It was just the sort of challenge that had always made Merry dig in her heels. She'd fought for the love of her aunt and for Colin, and surely in those losing battles she had learned enough to win.

"This time," she murmured, "will be different."

Chapter Four

"**I** think that's it for the day," Amy Galveston announced from the doorway to Merry's office.

Roused from her concentration on a patient's records, Merry sent the nurse a surprised glance. "You mean the waiting room's already empty?"

"Already?" Amy echoed. "It's after one o'clock. Saturday office hours are over and everyone else is gone. I'm starving, and I'm barring the door."

Merry laughed, knowing if another patient appeared Amy would be the last person to turn her away. A dedication to her job was just one of the many things Merry had come to admire about the petite brunette. Though they had worked together for just over a month, Merry already considered Amy irreplaceable—as a co-worker and as a friend.

"We've been so busy I lost track of time," Merry said, tossing the patient's folder on a stack of others just like it.

In the last three weeks, the patient load at the clinic had steadily increased.

Amy settled herself in a chair facing the desk. "I'm glad we've been busy, but I'm even happier that the rest of the weekend is free."

"Me too," Merry agreed. Response to the clinic proved just how much this facility was needed. However, she hoped there were no emergencies this weekend. She could use some time off.

"So what are you doing this afternoon?" Amy asked.

"Oh—things," Merry replied, trying not to sound too evasive.

Nevertheless Amy's green eyes narrowed with suspicion. "What things?"

"Just things."

Amy leaned forward. "One of those *things* wouldn't happen to be a trip to Sam Bartholomew's farm, would it?"

Searching for an excuse, Merry squirmed in her chair.

"I knew it!" With a frustrated gesture Amy slapped the arms of her chair. "Now, Merry, what did we decide—"

"*We* didn't decide anything," Merry returned. "*You* were the one who decided I should be a little more subtle."

"And I'm the expert on these maneuvers."

"And I keep telling you Sam isn't the sort of man who responds to maneuvers."

"Honey, there isn't a man alive who couldn't benefit from a little guidance," Amy insisted.

"Is that so?" a deep voice interrupted.

Startled, both women glanced up at the tall blond man who was leaning against the doorjamb, grinning. Dr. Jeff Cole had been making frequent, unexpected appearances at the clinic during the last few weeks. His interest in Amy was obvious, but to Merry's surprise the nurse didn't care for Jeff. Sparks flew whenever the two of them were together.

Merry watched with amusement as Amy squared her shoulders and answered Jeff's question.

"That's right, Dr. Cole. Most men require a great deal of direction."

One of his eyebrows cocked at the challenge in her words. "I don't know exactly what you're talking about, but I'm willing to defend my gender over lunch with two gorgeous women. How about it?"

Cutting off Amy's refusal, Merry said quickly, "I have other plans, but Amy was just telling me she's starving. I'm sure she'll be happy to have lunch with you, Jeff."

Merry ignored Amy's murderous glare and kept talking while she gathered up her medical bag and jacket. Jeff merely grinned, and Merry made a speedy exit from the clinic and into the crisp October sunshine.

She smiled as she turned on to the highway, happy to have given Amy a dose of her own matchmaking medicine. A few weeks ago Merry had made the mistake of casually mentioning her date with Sam. Amy had pried most of the story out of her, and since then the younger woman had been a fountain of unwanted romantic advice. It wasn't that Amy's credentials weren't excellent—she'd been engaged twice and never lacked for a date—but Merry suspected female trickery wasn't the way to rekindle Sam's interest.

Even as she repeated that observation to herself, guilt pricked Merry's conscience. On the seat beside her rested a box containing three dozen chocolate chip peanut butter cookies—requested by Sarah. Beside it was another box with a plastic model of the human brain—requested by Jared for a fourth-grade science assignment. If trying to get to a man through his children wasn't trickery, it was at least a close approximation. And Merry had been wooing Sam Bartholomew's children for nearly three weeks.

But I really do like his children, she told herself. Sarah was a lovable chatterbox. Jared was more reserved, but when encouraged he was full of questions about what it was like to be a doctor. Her interest in the children was genuine, and perhaps that was what kept Sam from telling her to stay away.

Not that she gave him a chance. Merry had managed her visits with Sarah and Jared very carefully these past weeks. The children were always around, and she was positive Sam wouldn't say anything ungracious in front of them.

After her Wednesday afternoon off when she'd first "happened" by the farm just as his children were getting off the school bus, she had waited for an angry phone call from him. It never came. And Merry thought he was unbending a little. If he didn't call, if he allowed her to come back into his home, then surely he wasn't as indifferent to her as he'd pretended since the night of the football game.

He hadn't been indifferent then. Hardly, Merry thought, her mouth going dry as she remembered her boldness in kissing him. There'd been desire in the lips that had moved against hers, reluctance in the steps that had carried him away. Surely if she kept spending time at the farm he'd drop the cool, polite manner he'd adopted. If only she could understand why he'd said they shouldn't see each other again. They were both unattached. She suspected he was lonely. She knew he was as attracted to her as she was to him. So what was the problem?

Asking herself that unanswerable question, Merry's grip tightened on the leather-covered steering wheel. The sight of Sam's mailbox, its fresh coat of paint gleaming white in the sunlight, forced her to relax. Getting all bent out of shape wasn't going to help anything. No matter what she'd told Amy, there was something to be said for playing it cool. Interested but not anxious—that was the way to get next to Sam. Taking a deep breath, Merry turned into the driveway, pausing as she'd done on most of her visits to appreciate the scene.

Like the mailbox, the house was newly painted. Big and white and boxy, it had nothing of real beauty to commend it. Nothing but a comfortable air of belonging, as if time had fused the house and the flat farmland into one. Discarded toys lay on the shallow front porch and a pair of bikes leaned against some untended shrubbery. The untidy touches didn't bother Merry. They suited a house that was full of life. By comparison, her own neat little house seemed sterile.

She pulled around to the back and noticed that Beth Kane was unpinning sheets from the clothesline. Sam's sister-in-law had been absent on Merry's other visits. Sarah had said her aunt was sick, and Jared had elaborated with the news that Beth was having a baby. While carrying her boxes from the car, Merry noticed that Beth did look pale and tired.

Smiling, Merry called to her, "Can I help you with that?"

"No need," Beth answered, and Merry wondered if the terseness of the words was intentional or due to the energetic way she was folding a sheet.

"Hi, Merry." The appearance of Sarah at the screened door of the back porch interrupted the exchange.

"Hi, sweetheart." Merry held out a box. "I made you the cookies I promised."

Sarah came quickly outside. "Can I have some now?"

"Don't spoil your supper," Beth called.

Since it was only a little past two, Merry didn't know how a cookie could interfere with a child's dinner. But she wasn't going to disagree with Sarah's aunt. "You can save them for after dinner."

As expected Sarah protested vehemently.

"Don't argue with Dr. Conrad," Beth said, the words punctuated by the snap of the pillowcase she shook out.

Merry opened her mouth to protest, wondering how she'd become the villain in this little disagreement. But her reply was cut short by Sam, his voice rough with annoyance as he stalked across the yard.

"What in the world are you doing?" he demanded of Beth. "I told you I would get the wash in this afternoon."

"You've got enough to do," Beth said, reaching for another sheet.

"I can handle it." With gentle firmness Sam took the sheet from her hands. "You don't need to be wearing yourself out like this."

"Don't be silly," his sister-in-law protested. "I'm almost finished anyway." Only a few sheets continued to bounce in the slight autumn breeze.

"I'll finish up," Sam insisted. "You go inside and take it easy for a while." Turning, he seemed to notice his audience for the first time. His nod was slight. "Hello, Merry."

She returned the greeting, hoping to melt some of his aloofness with the strength of her smile. "I brought some things for the kids," she said, holding up her boxes.

"And I can have a cookie right now, can't I, Daddy?" Sarah directed a furtive glance at Merry.

"As soon as you help me fold the rest of these sheets." Sarah grumbled until Merry leaned down to whisper, "How about two cookies?"

The child's frown vanished, and she scampered across the yard to help her father. Merry followed Beth into the house.

"Men get awfully protective at times like this, don't they?" She gave Beth a conspiratorial smile.

The other woman slumped into a kitchen chair. "What do you mean?"

"During pregnancies," Merry returned airily, taking the lid off her box of cookies.

"Who told you I was pregnant?"

The question was sharp, causing Merry to look up at Beth in surprise. "Jared," she replied. And why should it matter that I know? she added silently, noting the tense expression on Beth's face.

"I was afraid Sam—" Beth broke off, her face growing even paler.

Concern replaced Merry's faint aggravation. She took a step toward Beth's chair. "Are you okay?"

"Excuse me," Beth muttered before bolting into the small bathroom that opened off the kitchen.

Merry waited a few tactful minutes before going to stand outside the door. "Is everything all right?"

For an answer the woman inside issued a low moan and ran some water. Moments later the door opened to reveal an ashen-faced, shaky Beth. Merry grabbed hold of Beth's arm to steady her just as Sam came through the door.

He dropped the basket of laundry and was quickly at his sister-in-law's side. "What's wrong?"

Beth's smile was feeble. "Morning sickness—morning, noon and night."

"But nothing else?" Merry asked with crisp authority. "No cramps or pain or spotting?"

"No," Beth snapped, and with a show of renewed strength snatched her arm away from Merry.

"Remember that I'm a doctor—"

There was coldness in Beth's brown eyes and in her voice as she cut Merry short. "I have a doctor. A *good* doctor, thank you." Leaning on Sam, she made her way to the table.

Stung by the implication of the remark, Merry stood still, trying to think of something to say that would fill the awkward silence. Then, across Beth's bowed head, she caught Sam's imploring look. In his blue eyes was apology for Beth's thoughtless words. The look was enough for Merry. She said nothing. Instead she turned her attention to Sarah, who was standing in the doorway from the porch, frowning at the scene before her.

Merry crossed the room and stooped down beside the little girl. "Your Aunt Beth isn't feeling very well, but she'll be okay. Let's go outside and have a snack."

The box of cookies beside them, Merry and Sarah perched on a sun-warmed picnic table at the edge of the yard. Jared came from the barn and joined them. The sky was brilliantly blue. The breeze held just a breath of autumn coolness. Any other time, Merry would have been content. But she couldn't stop thinking about what had just happened with Beth.

Even considering the woman wasn't feeling well, it was clear she didn't care for Merry. Liza's death was the obvious reason, but Merry resisted that explanation. She didn't really know Beth, but the woman seemed intelligent, and an intelligent person surely couldn't blame Merry for something that no one could have foreseen.

Although, Merry reminded herself, it wouldn't be the first time she had been hated for reasons she couldn't control. She shivered, and in her memory rose the unmistakable smell of chalk dust and glue and the taunting voices of children who had discovered a new word and thus, a new weapon. *Bastard*, they'd called her, and the label had struck with all the force of a well-packed snowball. In their voices was childish scorn for anything and anyone who was the least bit different.

Different. Merry paused on that thought. That was probably why Beth seemed to dislike her. On the surface they had little in common. But if Beth got to know Merry, perhaps then she would realize they weren't so dissimilar. After all, they both wanted a home and a family. They both cared about Jared and Sarah.

I'll make her see we're more alike than she thinks, Merry resolved.

With such positive thoughts it was easy for her to call a cheerful greeting as Beth and Sam came out of the house. Merry joined them by the truck. "I hope you're all right, Beth."

Though he studied Merry's face for signs of malice, Sam could find nothing to suspect in the bright smile she gave

Beth. To his way of thinking she had every reason to be angry with his sister-in-law. Instead she appeared friendly and concerned.

As if beauty and brains and desirability weren't enough to prove Merry Conrad was something special, her sensitivity pushed her higher in Sam's regard. Dammit, he thought, forgetting he was attracted to her would be much easier if she weren't so nice.

Even Beth looked sheepish as she assured Merry she was fine.

"She may be fine, but I'm taking her home," Sam said.

Merry was quick to volunteer her help. "I'll stay here with Jared and Sarah."

"Are you sure?" Her eagerness surprised Sam. What was so attractive about an hour or so with his children? "Don't you have other plans?"

"Not as long as I'm not called to the hospital." She tapped the beeper on her belt.

"Okay. I'll be back soon." After admonishing the kids to behave themselves, Sam joined Beth in the truck.

Merry stood with one hand on Sarah's shoulder, waving as they pulled away. Like a man confronted with a "what's wrong with this picture?" puzzle, Sam kept glancing in the rearview mirror, trying to find a flaw. There was none. And that caused him to frown so deeply Beth asked him what was the matter.

"Nothing," he lied. Since the day in her kitchen when she'd voiced her doubts, Beth hadn't said anything to him about Merry. He didn't want to reopen the subject now. So for the rest of the drive he kept his eyes on the road, lest Beth see the longing he was certain showed in his face.

Longing? He almost laughed. The word was too tame to describe what he felt for Merry. For weeks he'd been reliving those moments when he'd held her. Her skin, soft as rose petals. Her scent, subtle as early spring. Just thinking about that kiss was torture. Knowing there would never be another was worse.

You're a fool, he told himself. A fool for wanting her. A bigger fool for letting her hang around the farm.

His anger had mixed with apprehension the first time Merry had appeared, saying she wanted to see Sarah and Jared. How was he supposed to forget her if she kept turning up underfoot? Yet during her visits she virtually ignored him. And instead of pleasing him, her coolness was an irritation.

How could she kiss him with so much heat and then ignore him the next time they met? Twenty times he'd started to call her, to ask her exactly what kind of game she was playing. Twenty times he'd hung up the phone without dialing. He was impatient with himself, not just because he didn't call, but because he was as eager as the kids to see her car in the driveway.

The eagerness of a man speeding on a dead-end street, Sam told himself. A no-win situation.

He tried not to think of Merry as he deposited Beth at home. Her husband persuaded Beth to take a rest, but Sam lingered, drinking coffee and talking with his cousin. His nerves were jumping, urging him to hurry home. For that very reason he took his time, and it was nearly five o'clock before he turned the truck down his own driveway.

The late afternoon air had cooled and Sam found the warm, lighted kitchen a pleasant contrast to the outdoors. Merry was poring over something at the table with Jared. Sarah was drawing a picture. From the stove came a spicy, mouth-watering aroma.

"Daddy! We're having s'getti." Leaving her crayons, Sarah ran toward him.

Sam swung her up into a bear hug. "Have you been cooking?"

She giggled. "Course not. Merry did. But I showed her where the pots were."

"She was a big help," Merry said. The smile she sent Sam's way was uncertain.

Before he could say anything, Sarah chattered on, "I helped Merry put up the sheets, and we washed the dishes and picked up my room—"

"And I did my room, too," Jared put in. "Then Merry helped me with my poster. What do you think, Dad?" Proudly the boy held up a cardboard sheet on which he had faithfully copied the brain and all its parts.

"It looks good, son." Sam's gaze traveled from the poster to Merry. The image of her washing dishes and picking up toys was hard for him to grasp, despite the well-worn apron tied over her slacks. In her soft gray blouse and diamond earrings Sam thought her too beautiful to have been doing housework, especially his housework. He couldn't help the suspicious turn his thoughts took. *Why is she doing all this?*

While he stood beside the table watching her, she looked away and went to the stove to stir the sauce.

Jared continued, "I'm gonna finish my report tonight while Merry's here to help."

Merry turned to the boy. "Jared, you can do that report by yourself. I won't stay for dinner."

The children protested, and on impulse Sam found himself echoing them. "Please stay. I mean, you made dinner. If you don't have other plans, you're welcome to join us."

Merry's hands twisted in her apron. "I hope you don't mind that I went ahead with dinner. You had all the ingredients, and Jared said everyone liked spaghetti."

"We do!" Sarah agreed as her father sat her down.

"Yes, we do." Sam rubbed at a tense muscle in his neck. Until this moment he hadn't realized how tired he was or how much he'd dreaded having to cook. "And I appreciate you fixing dinner," he told Merry sincerely. "I'm sorry I stayed so long at Bill and Beth's."

"How is she?"

"She seemed fine when I left."

"Good." This time Merry's gaze didn't waver under Sam's regard. He surprised her by smiling, the first real smile he had given her since the night they'd sat talking in front of her fireplace.

"Dinner will be ready in about forty-five minutes," she told him. "My sauce is better if it gets a good simmer."

"Great. That gives me time to finish up a few chores." Sam went out through the door to the porch but reappeared a second later. "Is there anything you need help with in here?"

Always a gentleman, Merry thought, even to the enemy in his camp. Suppressing a grin, she shook her head. But this time when he left, she went to the open door to watch him walk across the porch and the fast-darkening yard. Did she imagine it, or was his step unusually jaunty?

"Silly goose," she murmured, shutting the door and leaning against it. Touching a hand to her burning cheek, she stood there for a moment before realizing that Jared and Sarah were eyeing her with puzzled speculation. She forced her voice to remain cheerfully level. "Let's clear the table."

Maintaining an even keel, however, grew more difficult as the evening progressed. Merry couldn't decide which was the headier feeling—the warm sense of family that hovered around the table or the friendliness Sam displayed. For he wasn't stiff or distant with her tonight. He laughed frequently and always included her in the conversation. Whether his manner was an act put on for the children's benefit or not, Merry didn't care. She only knew that she liked him, liked him more with every moment that passed.

The four of them lingered over dinner and cleared the table together. Sam escorted a protesting Sarah upstairs for a bath while Merry helped Jared with his science report. Sam reappeared soon afterward and started filling the sink with dishwater.

Merry started up from the table. "I made the mess. I can clean it up."

"Thanks, but I know where everything goes."

Settling back in her chair, Merry returned her attention to Jared, but she was distracted by the sight of Sam, a dish towel tied around his middle as an apron. He wielded a dishrag as expertly as she'd expected him to swing an ax. And he looks damned good doing it, she decided. For the apron couldn't detract from the sheer masculinity of his broad shoulders and firmly muscled forearms.

He was drying the last dish when Sarah came downstairs clutching a dog-eared storybook. In a long pink gown and white bunny slippers, she was soap-and-water fragrant and eager to snuggle in Merry's lap. For a moment Merry closed her eyes and pressed her cheek against the child's soft curls. The gesture lasted half a heartbeat, just long enough for her to pretend this was her own child. The one she might never have.

The fantasy ended when she opened her eyes and saw Sam. Gone was his friendliness. Disapproval was as obvious as his frown.

Merry could see she hadn't made any progress with him at all. What would it take? she wondered, even as she began reading Sarah's book.

"It's bedtime for you two," Sam told the children after the story was finished.

"I have to go," Merry said quickly.

"I'd like you to stay a minute."

His expression made the statement much more than a simple request, and Merry didn't argue. She told both children good-night and waited while their father followed them upstairs. Standing in the suddenly silent kitchen, she wondered if it would be cowardly to escape while she had the chance.

In a feeble attempt to delay the inevitable, Merry started

talking as soon as Sam appeared. "I think Jared should get an A on this project of his. He's really very bright—"

"Merry—" Sam interrupted.

"I was surprised at how much he understands about the way the brain works—"

"Merry—"

She picked up the report Jared had left lying on the table. "Why, just listen to what he wrote—"

As firmly as he had taken the sheet from Beth earlier, Sam eased the report from Merry's fingers. "I'll read Jared's report some other time."

Merry swallowed. There was no use putting it off any longer. How bad could it be, anyway? He'd actually acted as if he enjoyed her company at dinner. Deciding she had nothing to lose, she forged ahead, "I guess you're going to ask me why I keep coming out here to see the kids."

He looked mildly surprised. Leaning against the table and crossing his arms, he paused before speaking. "Actually I was going to apologize for what Beth said this afternoon."

"Oh." Relief swept through Merry. "That was nothing."

"No, it was rude, and I'm sorry," Sam insisted. "Beth's not herself these days."

"I understand."

"You're sure?"

"I'm used to pregnant women being a little irrational," Merry assured him.

"Yes, I guess you are," he agreed, smiling.

Getting caught up in his smile is entirely too easy, she thought. When he was this relaxed and friendly, hiding her response to him was difficult.

"Merry?" he prompted, and his smile began to falter.

With a start she realized she'd been staring. *Get a grip,* she admonished herself silently, even as her cheeks warmed with embarrassment.

"I'm sorry," she mumbled, attempting to excuse herself. "I'm so tired I'm falling asleep on my feet. I think I'd better go."

Sam didn't hear Merry's words. He was much too busy watching the color bloom in her cheeks. He was trying not to imagine how that heated skin would feel beneath his fingertips. The impulse to touch her was so strong he clenched his hands into fists. He'd felt the same way when he'd seen Merry's sweet face pressed so lovingly against his daughter's hair. He'd squashed the feeling then, but here it was again. If he could just be in her presence and not think her desirable, he might have this thing licked. He'd tried during dinner to think of her as just another person, tried to forget she was a woman—

"I'll just get my things," Merry said, breaking into his thoughts. She turned and crossed the room.

Sam's gaze dropped, seemingly of its own volition, to the shapely curve of her hips. Masculine appreciation stirred. His body reacted. And he scolded himself, *You're worse than a twelve-year-old with his first girlie magazine.*

Still with her back to him, she shrugged into her jacket. "I told Sarah and Jared I'd come back to see them Wednesday afternoon," she said, swinging round to face him. "But only if it's okay with you."

He jumped and guiltily straightened away from the table, certain she could read his every erotic thought.

"Sam?"

"Huh?" Concentrating on her words wasn't easy, especially when he didn't dare meet her eyes.

I've embarrassed him, Merry thought. By gawking like an awkward teenager she'd put him on edge, and that wasn't in the plans at all. Sam had made it clear he didn't want to become involved with her. Knowing that, she had to ease herself into his life. When he saw how well she fit, maybe she could act on the attraction she was certain still lay between them. But she couldn't push.

Clearing her throat, she continued, "I hope you don't mind that I've been coming to see the kids, Sam."

Yes, I mind, he wanted to say, but he held back. Telling her that would be admitting she got to him. "It's okay with me," he lied. "But I don't understand why you're so interested in my kids when I...when we..." He faltered, trying to find a tactful way to bring up the scene on her porch three weeks ago.

"I know what you're trying to say," Merry interjected softly. They were headed into deep water, and she had to get them out. Striving for casualness, she explained, "I like your kids, and I like spending time on the farm. It's a treat for a city girl like me." The explanation wasn't the whole truth, but she reasoned that what Sam didn't know wouldn't hurt him. She only hoped she didn't look as guilty as she felt.

Sam searched her expression, trying to find a hint of falseness. There was none. Maybe she isn't playing games, he thought. Maybe the children really are the main attraction around here. She'd obviously taken him seriously when he'd said they shouldn't get involved. *And maybe that's my loss,* he thought bleakly, irrationally.

Impatient with himself, he hastened to answer her. "The kids like you, too. You're welcome to visit them."

"Thanks." Merry edged toward the door, anxious to get away. Half-truths and subterfuge didn't come easily to her. If she stayed much longer she would wind up telling Sam she was as interested in him as she was in his children. And that would never do.

She opened the door. "I really have to go."

"Drive carefully," he said, following her onto the porch.

The simple, usually meaningless phrase made her pause. How nice it would be if he really cared. Thinking that, she didn't dare glance in his direction. Instead she called a quick goodbye and walked to her car.

Sam stood on the porch while she drove away, wincing

at the squeal of her tires as they hit the asphalt of the highway. Lord, how he wished he could call her back.

The thought was a hopeless one, and he tried to banish it as he went inside. He had made sure she was no longer interested in him. At this stage regrets were pointless.

Yet he paused just inside the door and allowed himself to wonder what might have happened if he hadn't walked away from that kiss on Merry's front porch. Falling for her would have been the easiest thing he had ever done. But any relationship with her would never have lasted.

Since Liza's death he'd measured each day against its effect on the next. For that reason, temporary relationships held little appeal. And though he wanted Merry, wanted her with a fierceness he knew didn't happen very often, he wasn't willing to risk an age of heartbreak on momentary pleasure. Even if a woman such as Merry offered him pleasure on a silver platter.

The pleasure would tarnish, he assured himself once again. He'd fall in love with her, and she'd want to leave. It wouldn't be his fault. Sam knew he had a lot to offer, but he was certain Merry's expectations would eventually reach a little further than his simple approach to life could supply.

Sam shook his head and eased down in a chair. Except for the lights here in the kitchen, the house was dark. His gaze strayed over the familiar, shabby room. There were a hundred things he could do to keep from thinking of Merry. Any of them required more energy than his body could muster.

His mother would tell him to forget about being tired and go for a run. Sam smiled, almost hearing her voice. Exercise had been Eleanor Bartholomew's answer for dealing with frustration or anger or just plain heartbreak. Growing up, he had disregarded her advice. But the night she died he had raced across the newly sown fields and chased away the hardest, blackest edge of his grief.

He wondered how many laps it would take to erase Merry from his mind.

The straight wooden chair made Sam's back ache, but the pain was minimal when compared to the yearning in his gut. For a man who had been sure he didn't need a certain woman in his life, he was having some powerful doubts. What had he gained, except more nights spent alone? He had protected his heart. But what, in fact, was he saving it for?

The question chased itself around in Sam's head for hours, long after he'd gone to bed. He lay sleepless, searching for answers while the harvest moon did its best to crowd the lonely shadows from his room.

The clock beside Merry's bed showed 3:00 a.m. as she turned over yet again. Groaning, she sat up and switched on the lamp. She could actually hear her aunt's voice echoing through the moonlit room.

A guilty conscience will always keep you awake.

"Why did you always have to be so right?" Merry mumbled in reply. Shivering in the cool night air, she slid back down in the covers and let the guilt fold around her.

She had lied to Sam tonight. He had come right out and asked her why she kept coming to the farm, and she hadn't been straight with him. Evasiveness and game-playing had never been part of Merry's nature, and they didn't come naturally.

Throwing myself at him would have been a better approach, she decided. At least it would have been honest. Then he would have rejected her again and put an end to the whole situation.

Why Sam? she wondered. Why was she so drawn to someone who obviously didn't want her? She was just asking to be hurt. There were plenty of men in the world. If she forgot about Sam Bartholomew and looked about, Bingham, Indiana, probably had plenty of eligible males.

But do they have families? Merry asked herself. Do any of these nameless men have a little girl with soft chestnut hair? A little boy with a curious mind and a mischievous glint in his eye? Possibly, but the odds were against her finding another family just like Sam's.

Groaning again, Merry turned onto her side. Her mistake was losing herself in the fantasy of Sam and his children. He was the kind, sensitive man she'd never known. Jared and Sarah were the children doctors had warned she might never have. The three of them were Merry's childhood dream, the fruitless yearning of her failed marriage. They had seemed like a perfect picture, just waiting for her to fill the empty place next to Sam.

But Sam didn't want her.

And I might as well accept that, she told herself. She had to forget about him. Forget about the children. Forget about playing ridiculous games in order to carve a place for herself in their lives.

With that decision made Merry felt some of the tension ease from her body. Tomorrow she would see if Amy knew any eligible males. Tomorrow she would start forgetting Sam. Satisfied, she yawned and closed her eyes.

Only one thought kept her from drifting off to sleep. For Merry didn't know if she could ever, ever forget the way Sam's smile could reach all the way to his blue, blue eyes. And if she kept remembering that, how was any other man going to ever stack up?

She tried, however, to forget. On Monday night she went out with a friend of Amy's. On Tuesday she had lunch with a colleague of Jeff Cole's. Her only contact with Sam was the phone call she made to cancel her Wednesday afternoon date with the children. Her made-up excuse made her feel guilty, and Sam's deep, even voice made her waver. But she persevered.

By the end of a slow Friday afternoon she was miserable. Merry sat at her desk, staring out at the bright sunshine and wishing she could go to the farm and play outside with Jared and Sarah. Maybe Sam would join them. It was a perfect day to be outdoors, crunching through fallen leaves and smelling the trace of chimney smoke in the air. Jared and Sarah would probably play outside until twilight, and then they'd rush in for dinner, their cheeks red from the cool air.

What a fantasy, Merry told herself as she reached for a medical journal. What she needed to do was bury herself in work. The buzz of the intercom was a welcome intrusion.

"Call on line two, Dr. Conrad," the receptionist said.

"Thanks." Merry picked up the phone.

"Merry?"

The child's voice was unmistakable. "Is this Jared?" Merry asked.

"Yeah."

Pleased, she leaned back in her chair. "Jared, it's good to hear from you, but how did you know where to call?"

"Don't you remember? You put your telephone number on the bulletin board by our phone. You said we could call you if we needed to."

"That's right, I did." Concern creased Merry's forehead. "Did you need me for some particular reason? Is somebody sick or something?"

"Heck, no," Jared said. "But Dad told us you were too busy to come out here, and I wanted to tell you that my science project got the highest grade in the class."

"That's wonderful."

"Sarah wants to talk to you now," Jared said. "Thanks for helping with my poster."

"You're welcome, J—"

Her words were barely uttered when Sarah came on the line. Unlike many children who whispered shyly into the phone, Sarah almost shouted, "Why don't you like us anymore, Merry?"

In the background Merry could hear Jared telling his sister not to yell. The child ignored him and didn't give Merry a chance to answer.

"Daddy said you couldn't come to see us. Did we do something wrong?"

"Oh, sweetheart," Merry said, searching for the right words. "You didn't do anything wrong, but I'm..." She fumbled, searching for an excuse. "I'm awfully busy...."

"Too busy for us?"

I should have expected this, Merry thought. She knew people couldn't drift in and out of children's lives. Hadn't her own mother and a half-dozen "uncles" danced through her own first five years? She couldn't do that to someone else.

"No, I'm not too busy for you—" she began, and then stopped. How was she ever going to explain this to a six-year-old?

"Please come see us again," Sarah continued. "I'll be good."

"You're always good, but I—"

"Please." The word was a well-practiced wheedle.

As usual Merry melted. All her good intentions couldn't stand up to this little girl. "Okay, Sarah, I'll see you sometime next week."

"Oh boy!"

A crack sounded through the phone as Sarah obviously dropped the receiver in excitement. Merry could hear her chattering to Jared, and then the line clicked off. Slowly Merry replaced her own receiver and sat staring at the phone, deep in thought.

Even with their father and their aunt and uncle, these children had room for one more person in their lives. Maybe motherless children are always that way, Merry thought. Maybe we always have some leftover love.

At any rate, if Jared and Sarah wanted to see her, she wasn't going to disappoint them. They filled a hole in her own life. And Sam had said she was welcome to visit them.

Without her foolish romantic notions clouding the issue, maybe she and Sam could really become friends. And in that way, maybe she could share in the family she'd always wanted.

Sam could probably use another friend, Merry decided, thinking of the single parents she'd known in the past. With Beth having a child of her own he was going to need someone else to help. Quickly the idea of friendship with Sam turned from what Merry wanted to what Sam needed.

Ideas churned through her mind. Pictures of nice, friendly evenings with Sam and the children. Dinners at her house. Trips to the city.

Merry smiled, and with characteristic impetuousness she got up, jerked out of her white lab coat and grabbed her belongings. She raced down the hall, pausing only briefly at the front desk. "We're not too busy so I'm taking off a little early. Beep me if I'm needed."

Then she was outside, in her car and on the road to Sam's. The children didn't come running from the house as she pulled to a stop in the drive. They're probably playing in some distant field, Merry thought. Searching for signs of activity she headed for the nearest barn. Sam's truck was parked outside, but that didn't mean he wasn't out somewhere working.

She paused in the open doorway, peering inside. From beneath a large piece of machinery, there came the clang of metal against metal and a smothered oath.

"Sam?" Merry called, advancing cautiously inside.

Another clang. Another oath. A pause before he slid from under the machine, practically into her path. "Merry?" he said, his brilliant blue eyes peering up at her from a face streaked with grease. His checked flannel shirt, equally grimy, was open halfway to his waist. The inside of the building was well-lit, and it was impossible for Merry not to notice the mat of curling brown hair that covered his chest. Even from this angle, in these surroundings, the view was appealing.

All thought of friendship fled Merry's brain. All her plans to be a single parent's helper were forgotten. Her thoughts congealed into a confused mass and came out in one of those impulsive, confusing statements Aunt Eda Rue had so despaired of.

"Sam," Merry choked out. "I think you need me."

Chapter Five

*N*eed her?

As Sam savored the most obvious meaning of Merry's hasty words, his gaze flickered from her face and down her body. Slowly, deliberately, he lingered on her every swell and curve.

Need her?

He needed the complications Merry represented about as much as he needed snow in July. But damn—how many hot summer days had he longed for a January freeze?

He didn't need her. No, but wanting her was another matter.

His intense, assessing regard put a flutter into Merry's stomach. Why was he looking at her that way? "Sam?" she prompted.

Her soft voice sent red lights flashing in his mind. Dragging his gaze away from her, he pushed all the way out from under the piece of equipment and got to his feet. He managed to continue avoiding her eyes by wiping his face with a bandanna.

"That wasn't what I intended to say."

Sam stared hard at the dirty square of red cloth he crumpled in his hand. By contrast, he thought his voice was fairly smooth. "What did you intend?"

Studiously Merry kept her eyes off the masculine expanse of Sam's chest. "I honestly didn't intend to say anything. You startled me."

He just looked at her. Appearing nervous, Merry shifted from foot to foot. "Is there something you wanted?" he asked at last.

She cleared her throat. "Not especially. It's such a gorgeous day, I just wanted to be outside."

"Really?" He couldn't hide the skepticism that came through in that one word.

"Yes, really." Her shoulders squared. "I was sitting at my desk, wishing I were out in the sunshine when the children called—"

He looked surprised. "My kids?"

She nodded and continued, "But when I got here—"

"Why did my kids call you?" Sam pressed.

"I guess they missed me."

He frowned. "I'm sorry if they bothered you. I told them you were too busy to be—"

"I'm not too busy for them."

She sounded downright proprietary about *his* kids. His frown deepened. "You called Wednesday and said you were too busy. I figured it was the start of a trend."

"A trend?"

"Wasn't it?" Sam turned to the worktable that ran along the side of the building and began rummaging through some boxes. "You're a busy person, and even though you like the kids, you're going to have to disappoint them."

"Not intentionally."

The heavy metal chain Sam had lifted from a box

crashed to the concrete floor. Merry jumped, expecting to see anger on his face when he turned around. Instead there was a cold, steady blankness.

"I don't want to sound rude about this," he said. "But I'd prefer my kids didn't get disappointed too often."

"Because they've been disappointed enough?" she suggested.

"I didn't say that."

"But it's true, I think. I imagine it isn't easy being mother and father." Merry took a deep breath. "I was thinking today that you could probably use a break now and then. I guess that's why I said you needed me."

A pinprick of irritation flared within him. "So we're back to that, are we?"

Steadfastly she continued, "I think you need me to be a friend."

"A friend?" Sam repeated, wondering what kind of friend she wanted to be.

"Yes, I like your kids. I like spending time with them, and you could probably use some help now and then."

He was silent for a long moment, studying her features. They were beautiful, even features. Big, lustrous eyes. Small, straight nose. A generous mouth. A neat little chin. A face such as hers and the "Dr." she put in front of her name virtually guaranteed acceptance in a variety of places. Country clubs. Nice homes. Even Bingham, Indiana, had its share of the finer things in life. But she said she wanted to be his friend and spend more time with two kids on a farm. He didn't get it. There had to be a catch.

Crossing his arms, he leaned against the workbench, still studying her. "I'd like you to explain a few things to me."

"Like what?" Staying calm under his cool gaze wasn't easy, but Merry managed.

"I'd like to know why my children are so important to you." He held up a hand to stop her as she started to explain. "And, I'm sorry, but there's got to be more of a reason than that you just like them."

"But I do."

"Fine, but there's more to this." Sam hesitated, and finally gave voice to the suspicion he'd discarded last Saturday. "I hope you're not using the kids to get to me."

Her answer was an emphatic shake of her head. "Absolutely not, Sam. All I want from you is friendship." Sneaking another glance at his chest, she prayed she was telling the truth.

Sam again felt a stab of regret. He could have been more to this woman. But that wasn't the issue now. "Then why are you so interested in my children?"

Merry decided honesty was best. "Because I look at Jared and Sarah and I see myself."

"A kid without a mother."

His mouth set in a hard line, and Merry hastened to explain, "I'm not saying you don't do right by your children, Sam."

"Good," he said. "Because I do my best, and I don't think they're suffering for it."

Merry nodded in agreement. "You're right. They're wonderful, but they also need—"

"They have Beth," Sam interrupted, as if anticipating her next words.

"And Beth isn't feeling well."

"She'll be okay—"

"And when she is, she'll have her own child. What about Jared and Sarah then?"

The thought was one that bothered Sam a lot these days. The kids' physical needs he could handle. The house might not be spotless, but he could keep them well-fed and in clean clothes. It was the other part of the responsibility that daunted him. Between the farm and the house, when would he find time to check the homework, play the games and listen to the stories about school? True, he did most of that now, but Beth was always around to take up the slack, to lend another point of view. Merry was right, all that could change when Beth's child was born.

But Sam didn't want to admit he might have a need in his life for Merry. "I have plenty of friends and relatives who will help me out."

"Then why can't I be a friend, too?"

He couldn't answer. The reason why he couldn't be Merry's friend was tied to the way his insides turned to mush whenever she was near him. And anger was his only defense against this impossible attraction to her.

Merry continued, blithely ignoring his frown. "I probably have as much or more time to spend with the kids as any of your friends."

Sam allowed his impatience to bubble over. "You can't play mother to my kids," he bit out. "They're not a hobby you can pick up any time you're not busy. If you want children, maybe you ought to have some of your own."

He would have hurt her less if he'd slapped her. He saw that much in her face. In fact, the dull red color that splashed across Merry's cheeks resembled nothing so much as the imprint of a blow. As quickly as his anger had flared, it cooled.

"I'm sorry," she mumbled, stepping back. "I didn't intend to imply that I regarded them as a hobby. I guess I've botched this whole thing up. I'm sorry," she repeated, turning around. "Perhaps I should just go."

A small voice inside Sam suggested he let her leave. He didn't want her help and didn't want to be her friend. Mission accomplished, the voice said. Let her go.

But there was another voice. Stronger. More insistent. It sent Sam after her as she started toward the door. "Merry, I'm the one who's sorry," the voice made him say. "That was a really rotten thing to say to you, and you didn't deserve it." Then his hand closed on her elbow, and he turned her around to face him.

There were tears in her eyes. They trembled on the tips of her lashes, and they almost destroyed Sam. The impulse to kiss away those tears came from somewhere other than his brain. Only willpower held him back, even as his hands gripped both her arms.

"I was out of line," he said. "Way out—"

"Oh, I don't know about that," Merry returned and took a shaky breath. "Maybe you're not so far off base."

"No. I was." Satisfied she wasn't going to bolt for the door, Sam let her go. "You've been terrific to the kids."

Heaving a weary sigh, Merry sank down on the nearest flat surface, an overturned crate. "Yeah, I've been terrific to them. But what right did I have to do it?"

In answer, he merely looked at her.

"You didn't invite me into their lives. I just rushed in, the way I do everything. Aunt Eda Rue always told me to stop and think, and I—" Merry broke off and with the back of her hand, wiped at a tear that trickled down the side of her face. *Damnation, why do I have to cry?* "Oh never mind, Sam. I'm just going to go and leave you alone."

"No," he insisted. "I think you should stay and calm down."

The kindness in Sam's tone was what amazed Merry. She'd blown like a tornado into his life, but he could still be kind. Most men would be happy to see her leave. And the way he differed from the stereotypes would be reason enough for her to fall for him. Even without the intense blue eyes. Or the chest that was still very visible as he leaned against the wheel of a dilapidated tractor.

But, Merry chastised herself, she wasn't going to think of Sam as an attractive man. He was going to be just a friend. In Merry's estimation of friends, kindness counted a great deal, especially when mixed with strength. Since the first day she'd come to the farm, she'd known Sam possessed impressive amounts of both qualities.

"I didn't mean to upset you," he said now, softly. "But

I still have a hard time understanding why a woman like you would take such an interest in my family.''

"Someone like me?"

He shrugged. "A woman who's obviously very involved with a demanding career."

"That doesn't mean I can't love children," Merry protested.

"Why my children?"

"I told you part of it."

Arms folded across his stomach, he assumed a patient posture. "Tell me the rest."

Merry smoothed nervous hands down the front of her skirt. There was no easy place to start, except perhaps at the beginning. Her voice only shook a little as she began, haltingly, to explain. "My mother left me with Aunt Eda Rue and Uncle James right after I was born. Mother was beautiful. Wild. Impetuous. All the things my aunt hoped I would never be."

"Well, I don't think you're wild. She accomplished that much." Sam's grin grew into a full-fledged smile.

Encouraged, Merry continued. "Mother visited me from time to time. I thought that eventually she would take me away to live with her. I used to daydream about living with her in this big, brick house." She paused and drew a deep breath. "Like a real family."

There was a long silence as she stared down at the floor and shivered slightly in the late afternoon breeze that blew in the open door. "Mother stopped coming around when I was about five. But I guess I've always been on the lookout for that real family."

Merry held up her hand to stop him as Sam started to speak. "I'm really not trying to change your mind about our relationship, Sam. I'm in a new town, a little lonely, and I saw something, imagined something between us that wasn't there."

Then we've got the same vivid imagination, Sam thought, trying hard to concentrate on her next words.

"I still see a family," Merry was saying. "Your family. And I hope you've got room for one more friend." At last she looked at him again. "It would mean a lot to me to be your friend."

Even though common sense told him he could never be just her friend, Sam didn't know how to refuse such a request. He couldn't. He didn't ask what had happened to her mother or why she wasn't married with children of her own, but he suspected the reasons were painful. Perhaps being with his children would ease that pain a little. He liked the thought of easing Merry's pain. He liked the thought of doing much more than that for her....

He closed the door on those thoughts. Merry wanted to be his friend. She needed him to be hers. It seemed selfish of him not to try.

Mind made up, he straightened away from the tractor. "There's one thing we're going to have to get straight."

"What's that?" she asked, brown eyes widening.

"If you're going to hang around here, you're going to learn how to dress for the machine shed."

"How to dress?" Puzzled, Merry followed the direction of his gaze downward to her beige skirt. Black streaks zigzagged across the front. She jumped up from her perch on the crate. "What is this? Grease?"

"Probably just dirt—the same as you've got on your nose." Chuckling, Sam drew the bandanna from his pocket and came toward her. "Here, let me." Without thinking, he lifted her chin with his fingers.

Touching her was like igniting wildfire. Sam felt the heat as soon as it struck. So much for friendship, he thought, struggling to hide his feelings from Merry.

Thankfully he was spared the effort. The children chose that moment to burst into the shed. With voices raised in anger they doused any spark that might have lit between Merry and Sam.

"Daddy," Sarah said indignantly. "Jared said I looked like a mule."

"Did not!" Jared denied.

"Did too! Make him take it back!" Turning to Merry, the little girl shouted, "You make him take it back, Merry. Make him."

Above the children's squabbling heads, Sam's gaze met Merry's. "Okay, *friend.* Here's where you can start earning your keep. I've got work to do before dark." He flashed his perfect smile over his shoulder as he headed for the rear of the building.

Hours passed before Merry remembered that smile. Hours in which she settled the children's argument, helped throw together a quick meal and assisted in the carving of a jack-o'-lantern. Those hours were full, Sam was congenial, and there was no reason to think of him as anything but a friend.

But on the lonely drive home she thought again of that teasing, impudent smile. So unexpectedly easy and warm. So damned attractive. Just remembering it made Merry draw a deep breath.

And she wondered—bleakly—if friendship with Sam would ever really be enough.

In the weeks that followed Merry spent many hours at the farm with Sam and the children. And she had plenty of time to ponder the fragile line separating friendship from something more.

Merry approached each visit with an optimistic attitude, hoping this time she would finally view Sam with something that came close to casualness. But on every visit she was reminded that he was a man. A vital, interesting, intensely attractive man. Frustrated and yearning, she'd leave vowing never to come back. But, eternally hopeful, she always returned, only to be convinced again that her reactions to him were far too complex for mere friendship.

At times she thought he was playing a game with her. There was the night he emerged from his bedroom, barechested, shrugging into a shirt. His jeans had been unsnapped, too, and Merry was treated to a tantalizing glimpse of muscular chest and taut belly. He'd acted embarrassed and mumbled something about not realizing Merry was in the living room. But she'd been the embarrassed one, knowing he couldn't have missed the interest in her eyes. In fact she suspected he secretly enjoyed it.

She was positive he'd enjoyed the cold November Saturday when she had tried to build a fire in the kitchen's wood stove. She'd burned her hand and filled the house with smoke. The shrill alarm of the smoke detector summoned Sam from the barn. The mess had amused him, but Merry thought he took an inordinate amount of time and care smoothing a salve across her blistering knuckles. Not that she'd minded him holding her hand. But she thought something had lingered afterward—a look in his eyes, a gentleness.

He kept Merry off balance. One minute there was this tingling awareness between them. The next minute he was so carefully distant. In her confusion, Merry began to hope he had a flicker of interest in her as a woman.

She knew it could all be wishful thinking on her part. For despite her best intentions to the contrary, Sam definitely interested her as a man. Why else had she memorized every detail about him? The fresh scents of earth and air that clung to his clothes. The wave of chestnut hair that fell across his forehead. The width of his shoulders. The husky note of pride that crept into his voice when he spoke of his children....

There were a hundred details about Sam that Merry could summon to mind after having known him for less than two months. She realized, not without alarm, that her life was becoming hopelessly entangled with his.

She also knew there was one person who could separate them. Beth Kane. Even though the difficulties with her pregnancy kept her away from Sam's most of the time, Beth still did her best to interfere. She made no secret of her disapproval of Merry. It was in her voice when she called and Merry answered the phone. It was most certainly in her face on the one occasion they had found themselves together again at the farm.

As Merry sat and sipped a glass of wine in front of her own fireplace, she wondered about Beth's animosity. She was quite certain if Beth was feeling well, the woman would put a stop to the time Merry spent with Jared and Sarah. As it was, Merry suspected Beth was part of the reason for Sam's flip-flopping reactions to her. He always looked grim after talking to Beth.

"You'd think she'd be glad there's someone to give him a hand," Merry murmured, frowning as she stared into orange and gold flames. Then with determination she pushed Beth from her mind and stretched her jean-clad legs out in front of her. In a few minutes Jeff Cole was going to be on her doorstep, and Merry wanted some time to herself. It had been a tough week at the clinic and she was tired.

Even as she settled her head against the cushions of her couch, the doorbell rang. Grumbling, she left her comfortable seat, and as expected found Jeff shivering on the porch.

He grinned. "Hello, Merry. Sorry I'm late."

"Don't worry. The wine's chilled. The fire is blazing, and I'm all set to work out your romantic difficulties."

"The only difficulty is Amy's hard-headedness about something that happened two years ago."

Merry laughed and drew Jeff inside. "Come on in. My couch is open for psychiatric consultation."

Sam watched Merry's door close and felt as if a hot

poker had been shoved in his gut. When he'd parked here fifteen minutes ago, he'd never dreamed Merry could be waiting for another man. It shocked him to see her smile up at the tall, blond guy.

"The same way she smiles at me," Sam muttered. And the taste of jealousy filled his mouth like a bitter tea.

It had taken every drop of his courage to come to Merry's tonight. If it weren't for weeks of agony, he probably wouldn't be here at all.

Agony? No, more like hell, Sam decided. Ever since he'd made that crazy friendship bargain with Merry he'd been paying for it, paying every time she came near him. He saw her mouth and he wanted to crush it under his—kiss her until her lips were red and swollen and begging for more. Just the sound of her voice could bring instant arousal. The most casual of touches played havoc with his control.

And it wasn't just physical. Sam might have handled simple desire. But the way Merry's laughter filled up his home, the way she looked when she was with his children were in a whole different league of emotions.

Jared and Sarah certainly liked being with her. Sam had never intended to shelter his children, but he'd realized of late how he'd insulated them from other people. There was church and school, of course, but after Liza died he'd been determined to be everything they needed. Beth's help had been welcome, but he'd turned away the offers of well-meaning friends and neighbors. Now, with Merry, he could see how his son and daughter blossomed under the attention of someone other than family.

The children were why Sam was parked across from Merry's house, trying to find the courage to go inside. If she could love his children, wasn't she worth the risks of romance? He no longer believed Merry was interested only in his children. He had caught the looks she'd given him during the last few weeks. He couldn't ignore the tension that built between them whenever they were alone.

He still had his doubts, of course. He still didn't know if Indiana corn farmers should even dream of beautiful doctors. But for once Sam was determined not to worry about the future, especially since the present was so damned appealing. He'd worry about being hurt if and when it happened.

Besides, he told himself as he stared at the cheerful glow from Merry's windows, he had plenty to offer her. Passion. Laughter. A real family—exactly as she'd said she wanted. Beth was after him all the time, asking him why Merry spent so much time with the children, cautioning him about any involvement with her. But despite his sister-in-law's negative opinion, Sam thought he might just make Merry happy.

If he could just get rid of the blond guy in her house.

Smothering an oath, Sam left his truck, stalked across the street and up Merry's porch steps.

Warm air and soft music greeted him as she opened the door. Her mouth formed a surprised "Oh."

"Hello, Merry," he said, trying his best to smile. "I hope I'm not disturbing you."

"No, no, of course not." She stepped aside so he could enter.

In the living room Sam made no apology for interrupting and met the other man's eyes squarely. He found no answering challenge, only simple curiosity.

Merry made the introductions. "Jeff and I have been friends since I worked in Bingham before," she explained.

"Is that so?" Some of the tension eased from Sam as he glanced from Jeff to Merry. They certainly didn't look as if he'd trespassed on a romantic evening.

"Let me have your coat," Merry said to Sam. "Then I'll pour you a glass of wine."

"Thanks." He shrugged out of his parka.

Returning from the kitchen with a wineglass moments later, Merry was struck by the differences between the two men who stood in front of her fireplace. Jeff was tall, with the lean muscles of a swimmer. Sam was easily four inches shorter, but he dwarfed the other man. It wasn't merely the breadth of his chest and shoulders. It was presence. Sam was so alive, so vital that most anyone would pale by comparison.

And perhaps I'm prejudiced, she told herself while filling his glass with rich burgundy wine. Briefly she considered asking what brought him out tonight then discarded the idea. Merry didn't care why Sam was here. She was simply glad to see him.

Handing him his glass, she said, "Some people say red wine should only be served at room temperature. But I like all my wine chilled."

"In Europe they'd be appalled." Jeff left the fire and sat down in a cushiony chair.

"Well, this isn't Europe, and I'll do whatever I like." Merry refilled her own glass.

Sam frowned, even as he savored his drink. He'd never thought one way or the other about chilling wine, and a debate on the subject seemed silly. Who cared what they did in Europe? It was on the tip of his tongue to say so when he caught himself. For all he knew, this kind of talk was important to Merry. While Jeff told about a trip to the wine country of France, Sam let his eyes wander the room.

There was a subtle difference between now and the last time he'd been here. Perhaps it was the music. Before, Merry had put on a couple of old Beatles albums. Tonight the music was low and bluesy. It went with the wine and the soft lighting and the spicy aroma of bowls of potpourri scattered here and there.

The room was so very different from the familiar shabbiness of his kitchen. He thought it must be a relief to Merry to come back here after an evening spent at his place. This was probably the kind of evening she liked best—soft music, wine, relaxed conversation. This kind of

evening would keep her happy forever. An idea began to
form in Sam's head.

"Refill?"

He glanced up, startled from his thoughts by Merry's
voice. He smiled. "I guess I was daydreaming."

"Of something pleasant, I hope," she murmured.

Of you, Sam wanted to say. There was much he wanted
to tell Merry about his dreams, much he wanted to show
her. Now was neither the time nor the place, however, so
he contented himself with looking deep into her brown
eyes. For once, Sam hoped she could read some of his
thoughts.

Jeff coughed. "I think I should be going," he said.

"Do you really?" Merry said, turning from Sam.

"Yes, really." Jeff gave her a measuring look, full of
amusement and understanding.

She colored a little and tried not to appear too eager as
she retrieved Jeff's jacket from the foyer closet. "I'll talk
to Amy for you."

"I appreciate it," he said, suddenly serious. "I was confused two years ago, Merry. I'd just broken up with Karen.
Divorce isn't easy. You know that."

"Yes." Merry darted a swift glance at Sam. She had
never told him she was divorced. "I know."

With a last goodbye to Sam, Jeff was gone, and Merry
battled an attack of nerves as she turned back to the living
room. "He's trying to date one of the nurses at the clinic,"
she explained.

Sam nodded. "I figured that out."

"He's really a nice person—"

"Seems to be."

"And I'm hoping she'll—" Merry stopped, realizing the
pointlessness of the conversation. She clasped her hands
together and stared at Sam. He was still by the fireplace,
filling the room with his smile. There was something dif-

ferent about that smile tonight. Something that left her feeling a little breathless.

With movements she knew were jerky, Merry headed for the couch. "Why don't you sit down?" she invited.

"I'm fine here, thanks."

Again there was a long silence, and Merry had to tear her gaze away from the warmth in his eyes. Sitting down, she folded her legs underneath her and tried to relax. "Where are the children?"

"With some neighbors." Sam set his wineglass down on the mantel, took a deep breath and looked again at Merry. "I'm sorry about just dropping in."

"Why? I never need an invitation to come to your place."

"But that's different—"

"How?"

He shrugged, thinking he'd talked himself into a corner. "I don't know...the kids."

Merry smoothed a hand across the tweedy upholstery of her couch and wished Sam would get to the point.

"I was wondering," he began.

Her head jerked up. "Yes?"

He cleared his throat and offered a tentative grin. "I was thinking you might like to go out to dinner tomorrow night."

Like a sponge trying to soak up slow molasses, it took a moment for Merry to take in Sam's words. "Dinner?" she repeated, knowing her voice wavered.

"Yeah, tomorrow night if you're not busy."

"Well...sure. I know the kids—"

"Not the kids," Sam cut in. "Just you and me."

Expelling a long breath, Merry was silent.

The expectant smile disappeared from Sam's face. "Of course if you can't tomorrow, we can do it some other time."

"No. Tomorrow is just fine," she hastened to assure him.

"It's just that I'm—" Merry stopped, uncertain of what she felt. A month ago, Sam had said he wasn't interested in her. Now he was asking her for a date. At least she thought it was a date. He might be suggesting just an evening between two friends.

The warmth in his eyes dispelled that notion in a hurry. "I thought it might be nice to spend some time alone together."

She agreed with a nod of her head. She wanted to ask him what had caused this change of heart, but she realized there was no need for explanation. Actions spoke louder than words, or so her aunt had always told her. And Sam's actions told her he'd changed his mind. Did it matter why?

"I thought we might drive to Indianapolis," he continued. "If you're not on call, that is."

"No, I'm not. The city would be a nice change."

"Great." Now Sam's smile was broad and perfect. It dazzled Merry. "I'll pick you up about six-thirty, so we can eat about eight. It's a long drive, I know, but—"

"Six-thirty is fine."

"Then it's settled." He glanced at his watch. "I guess I should be going."

"It's not that late."

"I have to pick up Jared and Sarah."

Disappointed, Merry got up, retrieved his jacket and handed it to him in the foyer. "I'm looking forward to tomorrow."

"Yeah, me too," he whispered, wondering if his yearning showed in his voice. Merry was only inches away. One small motion could put her in his arms, the smooth, creamy curves of her body pressed against his. And if he made that motion every ounce of his control would snap. He didn't think he'd stop until they were upstairs, or in the living room, or any place where he could demonstrate just how much he could make her need him.

"Sam." The word was a sigh, a seductive net that pulled

him closer. He stopped it by stepping backward and opening the door.

"I'll see you tomorrow," he said, his voice husky.

Then he was gone. And Merry almost slid to the floor.

His effect on her couldn't have been more potent if he had kissed her. She'd wanted him to. God, she wanted him to do much more than that. And all because of one smoldering look from those blue eyes of his.

If a look could reduce her to this damp, throbbing ache, then the possibilities for more were mind-boggling.

Imagining those possibilities, Merry stood in the foyer, shaking, for a good ten minutes.

ing the door . . . .

Chapter Six

The tablecloth was damask, snowy white and satin
smooth. Silver, warmed by candlelight, rimmed the china.
And beneath the muted restaurant sounds was music. Low
and seductive. As intoxicating as the champagne Merry allowed herself to savor.

But not as heady as the smile Sam sent her from across
the table.

"I see you like the champagne," he observed.

"I love it." Leaning back in her chair, Merry returned
his smile and tried not to think of how much the bottle of
champagne must have cost. Her brain had been running like
a calculator throughout the evening.

For dinner Sam had picked a restaurant with that intimate, carefully understated atmosphere that always trans-
lates into money. Merry had been surprised when he'd escorted her through the door. Surprised but touched. For it
was obvious that he was trying to impress her.

He's spending a lot of money on something that's completely unnecessary, she thought. If she'd known what kind of evening he had planned, she would have...have...what? To even suggest they go somewhere less extravagant would have wounded his pride. Besides, he hadn't batted an eyelash at the prices. He looked as confident in a suit and tie as he did in a flannel shirt and parka. The only thing she could do was let him know his efforts were not unappreciated.

"That was a wonderful meal," she said, intensifying her smile. "Did someone recommend this place?"

"A college friend." Sam took a sip of his champagne, thinking of the late-night call he'd made to an old roommate who lived in the city. Greg had recommended the restaurant and prepared Sam for the prices. A lucky thing, too; otherwise he probably would have choked when he read the menu. But spending half of next month's feed bill didn't matter—not when Merry sat across from him, looking utterly at home and content in these surroundings.

He cleared his throat. "We could go somewhere else now, if you'd like. A movie or—"

Merry shook her head. "It's fine with me if we stay right here for a while."

"Fine. How about some coffee?"

After a waiter had poured them each a cup, Merry sent an admiring glance around the pastel-hued room. "This really is a gorgeous place, isn't it?"

"Yeah," Sam agreed. "It sort of puts the old farmhouse to shame."

"I like your house."

"I guess it has possibilities."

"I like it just the way it is."

He couldn't doubt the sincerity in her voice, and it amazed him. "What's so great about it?"

"Well..." Merry paused, visualizing the farmhouse. "For one thing it's old."

"Old and drafty and in need of a new roof."

"Not that kind of old." Cupping her chin in her hand, she gazed dreamily into the candles. "Old enough to have achieved character."

"Character?" Sam repeated, more interested in the gentle curve of her lips than her words.

"Just think of all the love those walls have witnessed," she continued.

"They've seen fights, too. You should have been around when my brother and I got wound up. We made Sarah and Jared seem tame, if you can imagine that."

"Believe it or not, I like to hear them arguing."

His laughter was full and hearty. "First my house has character and now you like it when my kids fight. You've had too much champagne."

"Well," Merry protested, laughing too, "I never had anyone to fight with."

"You didn't miss much."

"Oh, yes I did."

Her words rang with finality, and with them Sam saw the shadows creep into her eyes. The same look was there any time she spoke of her childhood. He reached across the table to touch her arm, his voice deliberately light. "You wouldn't sound so wistful if you'd been at our house on Saturday mornings. What a madhouse. In the winter Dad never made Mike and me get up early to help with the chores. We'd sleep till eight—"

"Really late," she agreed, knowing days at the farm usually began at dawn.

"Extremely late," Sam emphasized, continuing. "We'd always start roughhousing. Mike would swing a pillow at me, or I'd swing one at him. However it started, there'd soon be all-out war. We'd knock each other down and knock things off walls, and pretty soon Mother would be yelling from the kitchen...."

His words trailing away, Sam stared at a point above Merry's head. Just by thinking of those Saturday mornings he could smell the bacon frying and hear his mother's voice, half laughing as she came up the stairs to pull him and Mike apart. The memories were soft-edged and warm, like an extra blanket on a winter night. A person could grow cold without those sort of memories. The sort of memories Merry had missed.

With that thought, his fingers folded around the hand she had placed on the table.

"Maybe the next time Jared and Sarah start one of their fights, I'll have a little more appreciation," he murmured.

"Maybe you will," Merry replied, glancing down. How natural it was to see Sam's work-roughened hand against her own.

"Why don't you have a family, Merry?"

She looked up quickly, surprised by the question.

His grip on her hand was firm, his gaze steady. "You love children. You told me you always wanted a family. I think most anyone would wonder why you're not married."

"I'm divorced," she said, trying to sound matter of fact. "I thought you probably picked up on that last night when I was talking to Jeff."

"I guess I wasn't paying attention." Sam squeezed her fingers gently. "When you're around I sometimes have trouble concentrating on what's being said."

"Oh? And why is that?" Merry returned, imitating his teasing tone.

"I don't know." A grin tugged at the corners of his mouth. "I guess it has something to do with you being beautiful."

Though pleased at the compliment, she protested, "I'm not beautiful."

"Yes you are," Sam insisted, liking the flush that spread across her cheeks. "And whoever your ex-husband is, he must be a fool."

The vehemence of his words startled her. "I'm well rid of Colin Milsap, Sam. I was the fool for marrying him."

"You must have thought it would work out."

"Of course I did. I thought I could change him. He was divorced and famous for his pursuit of money and women." Merry swallowed, trying to rid her voice of its hard edge. "But I thought I could turn him into a perfect husband and father."

Sam searched her tightly closed features. "He didn't want children?"

She shrugged. "I don't think it really mattered to him one way or the other. Children were okay if they didn't interfere with his life-style."

"And what was his life-style?"

Merry decided to be blunt. That was the only way she could describe her ex-husband to someone as decent and good as Sam. "Let me put it this way. While I was in the hospital losing our baby, Colin was with another woman."

"Damn." For all its whispered brevity, the curse lost none of its venom. "How did you find out?"

"He told me."

Sam was amazed, not only by what she was telling him but by the anger her words aroused in him. Violent anger. Directed at a man he'd never met.

"I guess the truth was my punishment for asking," Merry whispered, remembering. Colin had been so cold, so cruel that day, smirking at her across the stark hospital room. She wondered now how she'd kept from striking him.

Her wounded expression tore at Sam's heart. "It wasn't the first time, was it?"

Merry's lips twisted into a bitter smile. "Colin turned cheating into a fine art."

"But you were having a baby with him?"

It was a logical question. But Merry couldn't give it a logical answer. Despite everything, she'd wanted her baby. Her impossible baby. She couldn't explain that to Sam. Not yet. She shrugged. "Maybe I wanted something to show for all the time I wasted hoping Colin would change."

"Someone should give him a taste of his own medicine."

Sam's voice was low and filled with fury. Instantly Merry regretted telling him about her ex-husband. She was no martyr to be admired for suffering through a bad marriage. "Colin was a cheat, but I made mistakes, too," she hastened to explain. "I stayed with him. I let him hurt me."

"Nobody asks for that kind of punishment."

Trying to make light of the whole story, Merry forced a smile and shrugged. "Well, I divorced him two years ago, and it's over and done with. I hardly ever think about him."

"Oh really?"

Her smile faltered under Sam's shrewd look. His eyes could see more than she would ever tell him. He probably knew she still cried over the unfortunate accident her marriage had turned out to be.

"You know, it's not a sin to admit things hurt," he said. "And some of those hurts don't ever heal."

The warmth of his gaze brought a genuine smile to Merry's lips. Gently he squeezed her hand. There was more comfort in that simple gesture than she had found in all the sympathetic murmurs of a dozen friends in Chicago.

"You know what?" she asked but didn't pause for his reply. "I think my memories of Colin Milsap are growing fainter by the minute."

"Good, because he doesn't deserve to be remembered."

"You're right." And for the first time in quite a while, Merry felt what had happened with Colin really didn't matter. He was history. Why worry about him when the future—and Sam—was right before her?

"Well, Mr. Bartholomew," she said, steering the conversation onto more pleasant matters, "now that you've plied me with champagne and discovered all my deepest, darkest secrets, I have a couple of questions for you."

Sam let go of her hand and settled back in his chair, smiling. "I'm an open book, Dr. Conrad."

"Really? Then tell me why you so suddenly decided we should go on an honest-to-goodness, for-real date."

The unfamiliar knot of Sam's tie seemed to tighten, and he fought the urge to loosen it while he searched for an answer.

She didn't give him much time before continuing. "Just a few weeks ago you were telling me you weren't interested. Now all this." She gestured to their surroundings. "This is more than just a dinner between friends, isn't it?"

He frowned. "Were you hoping that's all it was?"

The look in her eyes was heart-stopping. "I think you know better than that."

"You're the one who said we should be friends."

"Better friendship than nothing at all," she returned.

"Nothing at all would have been safer."

"If you feel that way, why did you ask me out?"

"I changed my mind," he said, the words sounding lame, even to his own ears.

"Just like that?"

"I straightened some things out in my head," he added. He hadn't really. Seeing Merry dressed in her silky blue dress in this elegant setting was a sharp reminder of the distance that still lay between them. Tomorrow it would be back to reality. And his reality wasn't soft lights, expensive wine and low music—things he was certain Merry required.

She gave him a measuring glance, wondering just what those *things* he'd worked out had involved. It was obvious he wasn't going to tell her, and it seemed a waste of time to keep asking. "I'm glad you had a change of heart," she said softly.

"Really?" He couldn't disguise the eagerness that lay behind that word.

"Tonight has been perfect."

I'd mortgage the farm again to keep her looking at me

like that, Sam told himself. Her eyes were full of magic, shining with promise. The look didn't falter as they lingered over coffee and dessert. And to Sam that look was worth every cent of the check and the hefty tip he left their waiter.

His confidence lingered as they started the long drive home. It was a cold November night, but the truck was warm. Cozy. As they rushed down the dark, nearly deserted highway, Sam felt closed off from the rest of the world. There were only him and Merry and the hard, bright stars overhead. No yesterday. No tomorrow. It seemed possible that he could go on driving forever, smelling her sweet perfume and knowing she was only inches away, wrapped in the soft luxury of a silver-fox coat.

The buoyant feeling ended, however, as quickly as it took Sam to realize his truck had a flat.

"Damn," he muttered, after guiding the vehicle to the side of the road and getting out to take a look. His flashlight shone on the right front tire.

Merry rolled down her window. "How does it look?" she asked.

"Flat."

"I know that." Her door slammed.

"It's freezing. Stay inside," Sam ordered, swinging the beam of light up to her face.

She blinked in the sudden glare.

"Sorry." He dropped to his haunches and examined the tire's rim.

Merry knelt beside him. "No real damage, right?"

"Doesn't look like it." With his hand under her elbow, he stood, pulling her up with him. "This won't take too long. Just get back in the truck."

"It's not that cold. I'll hold the flashlight for you."

"Don't be stupid. I can hold the flashlight." Leaving her, he opened the truck door and rummaged in the space behind the passenger seat.

"Don't *you* be stupid," Merry returned, joining him. "How can you hold the flashlight and change the tire?"

"I'll manage. Besides there's light from the emergency flashers. Get in and stay warm." Leaving the door open, he stalked with tools in hand to the rear of the truck.

"Oh sure," she said with sarcasm. From where she stood the dull red glow of the emergency blinkers didn't do much to illuminate the situation. She shut the door. "Get the tire, then give me the flashlight, Bartholomew."

"Merry, you're not dressed for this."

"And you are?"

"Merry—"

"Are you going to keep arguing with me or are we going to change the tire?"

"All right, all right." Dropping to the ground, Sam scooted under the truck.

"What are you doing?" Merry demanded.

"The spare's stored under here," came his muffled reply.

"Well for heaven's sake, let me help."

The thought of Merry stretching out on the dirt and gravel in her full-length fur coat was too much for Sam. He jerked up banging his head. "Dammit, Merry, don't crawl under here."

"But Sam—"

"I said don't," he shouted. "I'm doing fine." Smothering a frustrated oath, he jerked off his gloves and situated the flashlight so he could see to get the spare. Damn, but this wasn't the ending he had planned for this evening.

"Are you all right?" Merry called.

He bit back a sarcastic retort. Of course he was all right. He was just ruining his new suit. His expensive dinner was going sour in his stomach. And the woman he wanted like hell to impress was standing outside, freezing. What could possibly be wrong? Sam thought, freeing the tire with a vicious pull. He pushed it toward the end of the truck, slid out and found Merry by the tailgate, holding the spare with one slim, gloved hand.

"Give me that," he growled, too irritated to bother with politeness.

"If you give me the flashlight."

Sam made the trade with reluctance, and Merry followed him to the front of the truck where he set up the jack. In the dim light, she could see that his face was set in tense lines. Like most men, he was overreacting to a minor inconvenience.

"You'd think they could invent tires that wouldn't go flat," she said conversationally.

He grunted.

She tried again. "On the expressway in Chicago, I used to see these businessmen in their nice little suits with flat tires on their nice little BMWs. I always wondered if they knew how to change a tire."

"They probably picked up their nice little car phones and called the nice little auto club," Sam muttered, yanking the flat off.

Merry was silent, surprised by the fury in his voice.

"I guess that's what most of your dates would have done in this situation," he continued, shoving the spare tire into place. "Of course, none of them would have been out on a two-lane highway in a pickup, would they?"

"Sam, this is no big deal," she protested.

He wasn't listening. "Probably make a nice little story to tell Dr. Cole the next time he stops by to chat about his nice little trips to France."

Merry stooped down beside him. "This is just a flat tire. It could happen to anybody."

Not looking at her, he lifted the lug wrench and started securing the tire. She could see that his hands were red from the cold. "Where are your gloves?" she demanded.

He made a disgusted sound. "I can't change a tire with gloves on, Merry. Just hold the light."

"There's no reason to get mad at me! I'm just trying to help."

"Well, you're not helping," Sam retorted. "You should have stayed in the truck."

His tone sent anger crackling through her. "What is wrong with you?"

"Nothing is wrong with me. I just should have known tonight wouldn't work out."

"What didn't work out?" she protested. "I've had a terrific time."

"Dragging that fur in the dirt is a good time to you?" Pointedly he looked at the hem of her coat, which was pooled on the ground.

"I don't give a damn about the coat."

"Probably because you can afford to replace it. I can't."

"I don't know where you got the misguided notion that I'm hung up on material things," Merry said, acid in her voice. "I mean, I figured you were trying to impress me tonight, but—"

"Oh and this is really impressive, isn't it?"

"It's just a flat tire," she shouted back. "Would it have been less irritating if it had happened any other time?"

"Yes, dammit, it would have. Tonight was supposed to be special." Instantly Sam wanted to call the words back. He didn't need her to see how much it mattered.

"It would have been just as special if all we'd had was pizza and beer. I don't care about fancy restaurants, Sam."

"You sure looked like you were enjoying yourself."

"Because I was with you, not because of that overpriced menu!"

"Oh yeah." His chuckle was derisive. "I'm such an eligible catch—me and my farm and my kids and my bills."

Merry got to her feet, letting the flashlight clatter to the ground. "Just stop it! I'm not interested in your bank account or your credit rating or the kind of car you drive. If those things mattered to me I wouldn't have gone out with you in the first place."

"Well, why did you come?" Sam demanded, jumping up.

"Because you're real." Merry grasped him by the shoulders and gave him a little shake. "Because you're not hiding behind some suit or some fancy title. You're rock solid, the same today as you were yesterday, the same as you'll be tomorrow. If you'd listened at all to the things I've said to you, you'd know that's what matters to me."

Sam heard the words, and for a moment they made sense. It wasn't money or possessions that Merry had talked about tonight. Or at any time, for that matter. She talked of children. Of a home. The simple things he took for granted. If he listened only to what she said, he could almost believe she'd fit into his life. Almost.

"Those are very fine words," he began. "But—"

"But what?" she cut in. "You don't believe them? Well, believe this."

Before he could protest, she kissed him, instinctively finding his lips even in the dim light of the emergency blinkers. His face was cold, and his mouth was unresponsive. But she wasn't giving up. Pressing her cheek against his, she whispered, "Damnation, Sam. This is the second time I've had to kiss you. When are you going to get with the program?"

"Merry, this is crazy."

"Just shut up and kiss me. That's all I care about."

"You say that now—"

"What's wrong with now?"

Her breath was warm against his skin, and Sam spared half a second to savor it before his lips found hers. It was no good pretending her kiss didn't move him. With her in his arms, he could believe anything. The doubts and fears fell away, leaving him with passion. Hard and direct, the feeling could consume him if he wasn't careful.

But he didn't want to be careful. Not now. Not while Merry was this close.

A truck passed, horn blaring, bathing them in a frigid breeze and the stink of exhaust. Sam ignored it. He shut his eyes, trying to forget they were beside a cold, wind-swept highway. On Merry's mouth he could taste his own need. Hot, undiluted desire. The sensation thrust the last of his hesitation aside. Groaning, he combed his hand through her hair, cupping the back of her neck as he pulled her closer.

"Your hands are cold," she murmured when at last they broke apart.

"I'm sorry." Quickly his arms went around her again, this time beneath her coat. "Maybe you can warm them up."

"Maybe," was all she could say before he was kissing her again. And touching her. On her back his hands slid down the silk that separated them from her skin. Merry thought they must be leaving a mark on her, a scalded imprint. When they slid farther and cupped the rounded curves of her hips, she was certain he had branded her forever.

Long moments passed before they parted again. Endless minutes in which she imagined the heat of their embrace had melted everything standing between them and the future. But the still rational part of her brain knew the finer points of a relationship couldn't be smoothed away with kisses, no matter how fevered or breathtaking.

His lips left hers slowly. But their bodies were still molded together, cocooned from the cold wind by her opened coat. Against her ear, his voice was little more than a shaky sigh. "I guess that's been coming for a long time."

"I know I've given it a lot of thought."

"Did it live up to your expectations?"

"Surpassed them," she murmured, leaning into his strength. His arms felt so good around her.

In a lazy motion, his hand trailed up her back again. "We're so different, Merry. I'm just not..." He paused, sounding as if his words were hard to choose.

"We're not that different, Sam."

"But I'm—"

Her hand closed over his mouth, stopping the words she knew he was going to say. "You're a very, very special man, Sam Bartholomew. I saw that from the beginning. Do you think I'd waste my time on someone who was less than I wanted? I've wasted half my life already."

If he could just hold on to this feeling, Sam thought. If he could just shake the certainty that Merry would someday walk out of his life as abruptly as she'd entered it. He had to stop worrying about that. Last night he'd decided to take a chance on her. And here she was—in his arms. He was going to concentrate on how very right that felt.

When Merry's hand fell away from his mouth, he said, "Okay, what do we do now?"

"Maybe we should just approach this the way any farmer would."

"How's that?"

"We give it some time and attention and see if anything grows."

How could he resist the husky undertone of her voice? Sam leaned forward. "I suppose this crop will need plenty of cultivation."

"Lots and lots," she said before her lips opened beneath his again.

Holding his reactions closely in check, he pulled away before the kiss could deepen. "If we keep this up, you may get more of a crop than you can handle."

"I'm game if you are."

His entire body tightened. If she only knew how desperately he wanted to plant himself deep, deep inside of her. But it was too fast. Too soon. He had to get control of the situation now. "We could freeze out here, you know," he said, trying to lighten the mood.

"My feet maybe—every other part of me is very warm."

He ignored the implications of that remark. "Then I think we should finish getting this tire changed and warm up your feet."

"I guess you do need to be getting home, don't you?"

"I'm already an hour late."

"Okay." Acquiescing gracefully, she stepped back, and the frigid wind slammed into her. She shivered. "It is cold."

"Freezing," Sam agreed. "Now come hold the flashlight while I fix this tire."

Merry laughed. "Just listen to who's asking for my help now."

"Kisses always make me mellow."

"I'll have to remember that."

The tire was soon changed and they climbed back into the truck. Merry found it difficult to face Sam in the lighted cab. Outside the darkness had been a shield. Now she couldn't avoid his eyes. Those deep blue eyes could see everything, including the insecurities she tried so hard to hide. Because for all her brave words, Merry was afraid. Every time she'd tried for a piece of heaven, it had always slipped away. And something told her Sam was her last chance.

Surprisingly he seemed to find the confidence she had lost. His hand closed around hers. "I never thought I'd be so grateful for a flat tire."

"Kind of cleared the air, didn't it?"

He grinned. "Yeah. Otherwise, I might have continued taking you to restaurants I can't afford. You could have ruined me."

"I guess it's burgers and pizza for a while, huh?"

"More like beef stew and spaghetti at my place."

"Hey, I live for tomato sauce."

Her hand stayed in Sam's almost all the way home. That was a secure feeling. Yet as the miles rushed by she couldn't rid herself of the premonition that most of their troubles lay straight ahead.

In the morning Merry's uneasiness seemed foolish, especially since a phone call from Sam awakened her.

"You were still asleep," he accused after she'd mumbled a groggy hello.

Groaning, she rolled over and eyed the bedside clock. "Of course I was still asleep. It's not even six-thirty."

"High time you were up."

"Don't tell me you've been up for hours."

"No, not hours," he said, laughing. "I'm sorry I woke you, but I wanted to call before the kids got up. They'd want to talk if they knew it was you on the phone." His voice dipped lower. "And I want you all to myself."

With his last words, a flutter of happiness settled in Merry's stomach. She snuggled deeper under the covers. "You could talk like that all day. I'll just lie here and listen."

"Wouldn't you rather come and have breakfast? I'm cooking the usual Sunday morning pancakes."

"With lots of butter and maple syrup?"

"And bacon on the side."

She sat up, pushing a hand through her tousled hair. "Can I have an hour to get dressed and get there?"

Sam sighed. "I don't know if I can wait that long to kiss you again."

Not taking time to shower, Merry made it to the farm in just over thirty minutes.

After that Sam called her every morning before the children were up. As he sat talking on the phone in his darkened kitchen, Merry's sleepy voice created an intimate feeling. Their talks were brief and of everyday matters. The weather. One of her patients. Whether or not he should buy a new tractor. When he hung up, however, he felt as if they'd discussed something very important. Those quiet conversations put a spring in his step as he went upstairs to rouse Jared and Sarah. The feeling of happiness lingered and kept Sam going until he saw Merry again.

He lived that way—from one moment with Merry to the next. Day by day. Not looking backward or forward.

They were together as often as possible. Some nights she came out to his house and had dinner with him and the kids. They went to her house a few times. The farm wasn't busy, so he came into town often and had lunch with her. They usually ate in her office, staring into each other's eyes and stealing kisses behind the closed door.

It grew harder and harder to be content with kisses. In his arms, Merry was sweetly, unmistakably willing. But he hesitated to take their physical relationship any further. It had to be the right moment. He had to be sure of his feelings. Of hers. To Sam, making love was the ultimate commitment and only part of any relationship. So every night they separated, he ached from wanting her.

He didn't need anyone to add to his uncertainties, but his sister-in-law always did.

Although her doctor was watching her blood pressure and advising as much rest as possible, Beth was feeling better and was again spending more time with Jared and Sarah. Sam didn't mind. They loved their aunt. But Beth didn't trust Merry, and since Merry was now part of Sam and the children's lives, there was friction.

Beth's interferences were small and sometimes hard to detect. A critical remark about an outfit Merry bought for Sarah. A disapproving sniff when Jared said Merry had come for Sunday breakfast. A sour look when Sam kissed Merry goodbye.

"Goodness," she told him after Merry had left one night. "You act as if she's going to get tired of you and never come back."

To himself Sam admitted to being afraid of just that. To Beth he directed a plea for patience. "If you'd just give Merry a chance, you'd really like her."

His sister-in-law's answering look was skeptical, and so were Sam's hopes for winning her approval. Knowing her stubborn nature, he thought pushing her would do more harm than good. So he sat back and hoped for the best.

Merry said nothing about Beth's attitude, even though Sam knew she caught every subtle criticism. And with some hesitation he invited Merry to the family Thanksgiving dinner.

Since Liza's death Sam had celebrated the holiday with Bill's family. Bill's mother was quite a cook, and with several other cousins to help her she always put together an impressive spread of food. The day had a pre-set pattern. They always ate at one. The men retired to the living room to watch football. The women did the dishes and sat around the kitchen table, drinking coffee and talking.

Merry fit in with the family better than Sam had hoped. No one gave him a what's-she-doing-with-you? look. By the time dinner was over he was completely relaxed, proud of Merry's beauty, her sense of humor and even her football knowledge. He didn't mind that she was the only woman in the living room watching football and didn't catch the significance of it until later.

Merry brought it to his attention that night after the kids were asleep and the guests had left. "Beth threw me out of the kitchen," she said bluntly.

"Threw you out? Now come on, Merry—"

"It was all very nice and very polite, but she threw me out just the same, Sam." Tears of fury welled in her brown eyes.

Sam couldn't stand her tears. Sitting down on the couch, he pulled Merry onto his lap. He settled her head on his chest, liking the feel of her soft hair against his chin. "What did she do?" he asked finally.

Taking a deep breath, Merry began, "Just forget about it."

"No. You're upset and I want to understand why."

She wondered if she could ever explain the subtleties of the situation to him. Men as often didn't understand these sort of things. "All the women were in the kitchen, Sam. Talking about women things. It's not that I think they should have been in the kitchen. It's kind of an archaic tradition."

He grinned, knowing Merry's view of anything that smacked of inequality. "So what did it matter if you weren't included?"

"Because I wanted to be in there. I wanted to feel like part of the family. But Beth didn't want me there. She said I'd be more comfortable in the living room, that I was a guest, that I should go find you to entertain me. I felt like such an outsider."

It crossed Sam's mind that she was an outsider, as different from those other women as he was from the friends Merry had left behind in Chicago. But he couldn't say that to her. "What did everyone else do?" he asked.

"Beth was very nice about the whole thing. I'm sure everyone else thought she was sincere. But she was pushing me away, and I couldn't do anything about it without causing a scene."

Sam tried to think of some way to explain Beth's actions. "Are you sure she wasn't really trying to make you feel more comfortable?"

Sitting up, Merry snorted. "Oh give me a break. Beth hates me. She didn't want me at that dinner today. And she doesn't want me in your life."

"I think hate is too strong a word. Just give her some time. She's not herself—"

"It's not fair to keep blaming all this on her pregnancy. She just doesn't like me, Sam, and I think she's turning the kids against me, too."

Now he sat up straighter, concern tightening his features. "What are you talking about?"

"Surely you've noticed the way Jared rebels every time I ask him to do anything."

"He gets a little hard to handle sometimes. That has nothing to do with you."

Merry's eyebrows cocked at a skeptical angle, and Sam's certainly faltered a little.

"Okay," he admitted. "Maybe Jared is a little jealous of the time I'm spending with you. Up until now they've had me all to themselves."

"It's more than that," she countered, shaking her head. "Even Sarah is pulling away."

"Well, maybe she's jealous, too. You started out being just her friend. Now she sees us together. You know she was a little surprised the first time she saw us kiss."

Stubbornly Merry refused to accept his explanation. She knew it was more than that. Much more.

"Beth wouldn't use the children," Sam insisted.

"Maybe she doesn't realize what she's doing."

"Oh come on." Irritation carved lines beside Sam's mouth. "You're blowing this way out of proportion."

The last thing Merry wanted was to fight with him over Beth. If that happened, the woman would have succeeded in driving a wedge between them. Merry wasn't going to give her that satisfaction.

"Maybe you're right," she conceded and settled back against Sam's broad, comfortable chest. Inwardly she was anything but convinced.

"I'm sure of it." His fingers cupped her chin, bringing her mouth up to within inches of his own. "Besides, don't we have better things to do than talk about Beth?"

"Do we?" Her words were silenced by his lips on hers. *How quickly he can make me forget everything but his touch,* Merry thought.

His kiss was always this way. A match strike of sensation, leaving her hot and moist and yearning. Her mouth parted under the pressure of his, and he deepened the kiss, edging her downward. As they stretched out on the couch, his hand moved from the curve of her waist to the underside of her breast. A sound, part sigh and part groan, came from her throat as his thumb rubbed gently upward to finally caress the hardening tip.

"Merry," he whispered against her mouth. "Ah, Merry," he repeated as his hand slid downward and then up under her sweater. In mere seconds, with a minimum of fuss, her breast filled his hand. And arousal burned its way through the rest of her body.

She knew Sam was just as shaken. His lips were hungry on hers. She could feel his heart pounding furiously. And pressed against her hip was the unavoidable proof of how she affected him. She shifted, her fingers moving toward the buckle of his belt.

Leaving her breast, his hand intercepted hers. "Wait," he said, pulling away. "Merry...wait..."

"But Sam—" she protested.

"Just wait," was all he said before gathering her close.

He held her that way until his breathing slowed and her own heartbeats resumed a semblance of normalcy. By the time Merry slipped out of his embrace and adjusted her clothes, they were both in control of themselves.

It was all she could do to keep from asking Sam why he had stopped. Perhaps it had something to do with the children sleeping just one floor above them. Perhaps it was something deeper. In any case, though Merry's innate confidence had allowed her to pursue Sam, she couldn't ask him to sleep with her. She knew the right time would come.

But it didn't help her patience that she could still taste desire in his parting kiss.

Chapter Seven

With December came another blast of cold air and a winter storm that turned the streets to ice. Road crews worked overtime clearing the way, but Merry didn't make it out to the farm for a couple of days. She missed not playing in the snow with Jared and Sarah. She didn't think they missed her.

Standing at her office window days after the storm, she tried to reassure herself. "It's just as well we have a little time apart," she murmured, and watched an icicle break off from the edge of the roof. Today the sun had melted most of the snow, leaving patches of ice to glitter in the parking lot like fragments of a broken mirror. Pieces of bad luck, Merry thought, shivering. Deliberately, she turned away from the wintry scene.

Turning away from her troubling thoughts was not so easy. Her relationship with the children had deteriorated rapidly since Thanksgiving. Jared was the real problem. He was hostile and rude, and Sarah—sweet loving Sarah—was following her big brother's lead. Sam still insisted it was jealousy and thought they'd get over it. But the night before the snowstorm he had punished both children for being rude to Merry. She wouldn't soon forget the accusing, angry glare Jared had given her before being sent to an early bedtime. With so sour an expression the boy looked just like his Aunt Beth.

Merry still thought Beth was somehow behind the change in the children. They'd been just fine until the woman had resumed her frequent visits to the farm. If only Sam could see what his sister-in-law was doing.

He couldn't, though. He admitted Beth didn't like Merry, and he thought Jared and Sarah could be picking up on the woman's negative feelings. However, he refused to consider that Beth would ever say anything outright to influence the children. Merry disagreed, but she kept her opinion to herself. To do otherwise only made Sam uncomfortable and angry.

She only wished she could understand why Beth had it in for her. Didn't she want Sam to be happy?

And I can make him happy, Merry told herself with quiet certainty. In the last few weeks, she and Sam had grown closer. With her he opened up. He talked more, laughed more easily. He shared his hopes, his fears, his dreams. Sam needed her. And filling that need might have been enough for Merry, even without the sensual current running between them.

Her cheeks burned as she thought of the way Sam made her feel. She understood arousal, had experienced it before. But never like this. Just the thought of him touching her sent a languid, liquid feeling through her body. Thinking about him now, her knees went rubbery, and she quickly sat down at her desk.

His holding back only heightened the tension. Like a dieter given only a nibble of chocolate ice cream, a taste of ecstasy only whetted the appetite.

Why was he hesitating? Merry had asked herself this question dozens of times since the evening he'd taken her to dinner. And finally she'd decided even this had something to do with Beth.

Merry knew Sam worried about the differences between his life-style and hers. He was quick to think she wasn't satisfied with a quiet evening at home or was bored spending so much time with the children. Beth exaggerated those differences by constantly drawing attention to them. Or so Merry thought. She couldn't find another explanation for why Sam didn't take their relationship to its next logical step.

Talking to him about it might easily give her the answers. But so far Merry hadn't found the courage. Should she be subtle or come right out and ask him why he wasn't moving forward? It wasn't a question Merry had ever been forced to ask. Until now, her problem had been keeping men out of her bed—not enticing them in.

"Which is a problem many women might be pleased to have," Merry mused aloud. Perhaps she should consider herself lucky and be patient. But even that thought didn't erase her anxiety, and the problem continued to nag at her until the afternoon office hours began.

Her schedule was full, and the rest of the day passed quickly. At five o'clock she was surprised to see the office staff making their exits behind the final patients. Like most days, she and Amy were the last ones left in the building.

"Wait a minute," Amy called as Merry turned down the hall. "Looks like another appointment just showed up."

Through the glass in the reception area's door, Merry could see Sam coming up the front walk. He wore a parka and jeans, and as usual she was struck by his clean-edged good looks. She reached the door just as he opened it, and the air that rushed inside brought the damp smell of melting snow and Sam's own masculine, outdoorsy scent.

"Hello, stranger," she said, a breathless, happy catch in her voice.

"Hi, yourself." His smile reached all the way to the crinkles beside his blue eyes.

At the reception desk Amy stifled a giggle. "I hesitate to interfere, but you two are letting the heat out."

Feeling his face color slightly, Sam allowed the door to shut behind him. "Hello, Amy," he said, giving the brunette nurse a nod.

"Nurse Galveston, don't you have somewhere to be?" With mock severity Merry turned toward her friend.

"I'll go count cotton swabs or something." Grinning, Amy disappeared down the hall.

Sam watched her go with amusement. "Any luck with her and Dr. Cole?"

"Some," Merry said, looping an arm through his as they crossed the room. "But it's not very interesting. I'd rather talk about how much I've missed you."

Drawing her round to face him, Sam's hands slid up to her shoulders. Damn, but he'd missed the feel of her. "You could have come out to the farm and been snowed in with me."

Her heart quickened at the thought. "You always have these great suggestions after the fact," she accused, raising her lips to accept his kiss.

As he stepped back, his hands framed her face, and he savored the tender look in her eyes. That look could chase every doubt from his mind. "Sometimes I forget how beautiful you are," he whispered, and his thumb flicked across her lower lip.

She drew a shaky breath. "You're not so bad yourself."

His hands drew her toward him again. His voice lowered. "You're just flattering me so you can take advantage of me later."

Making a soft sound of agreement, Merry ran her hands under his parka and across the nubby texture of his sweater.

The material was warm, and it wasn't much of a stretch to imagine the heat of the skin beneath. Touching that skin would be heaven.

"Daddy?"

The softly spoken word jerked Sam away, and silently he cursed himself for feeling guilty. In the doorway were Sarah and Jared. Between them was Beth.

"Hello, kids," Merry said brightly, trying to fill the awkward pause.

Sarah's answering smile was as genuine as they came, but after a quick glare from Jared, she scowled.

Looking from Sam to Merry, Beth's brows drew together in a frown. "I hope we're not too early."

"Of course not." Sam leaned forward to tousle Jared's hair.

Merry, perched on the edge of the reception desk, wished the boy would at least look at her. "Early for what?"

"I thought we might all go out for pizza," Sam answered.

"All of us?" Merry's gaze swung up to Beth, and too late she realized the reluctance her voice betrayed. "I mean," she amended quickly, "that should be fun."

Beth laughed, a sound totally devoid of mirth. "I'm just delivering the kids. I took them to a birthday party on the other side of town this afternoon."

"A birthday party?" Merry seized upon the subject to cover the rush of anger Beth aroused in her. "Did you have fun, Sarah?"

Forgetting to be distant, Sarah nodded in excitement. "We had cake and ice cream and games and presents and—"

"A perfectly ordinary kid's party," Beth interjected. "Not something you'd be interested in, Merry."

"Beth..." Sam began, his voice full of warning.

They're going to have it out, Merry thought, glancing in alarm from one to the other. She thought Beth deserved to be taken down a notch or two but not in front of the kids. "Sarah," she said quickly, sliding off the desk. "Would you like to see my office?" At that moment Amy appeared in the doorway from the hall. "Look Sarah, this is Amy, she can show you where I work. I put some of the pictures you drew up on my wall...."

Amy flashed Merry a puzzled look, but she took the cue and held out her hand. "Come on, Sarah. Merry has a jar of candy on her desk. We'll go have some."

For candy Sarah could be induced to do almost anything. The nurse's gamine smile cinched the offer. Sarah took Amy's hand and disappeared down the hall.

"Jared," Merry prompted and started forward.

"No," he said, hanging back. "I'm not going with you."

His father gave him a little push. "Go on, son. I want to talk to your Aunt Beth."

"No, I'm not going with Merry," Jared shouted, clutching at Sam. His next words seemed to bounce off the walls. "She killed my mother."

"Jared," Sam whispered into the sudden silence.

From Beth there was a shocked gasp.

Merry felt as if the room tilted.

"Why'd you do it?" Jared yelled at her, his voice coming from a long distance away. "Why'd you kill my mother?"

"Stop it, Jared!" Sam ordered. "Merry didn't kill anyone. Where in the world did you get an idea like that?"

Tears welled in the boy's eyes. "Aunt Beth told me. She said Merry was there when Mother died."

As all eyes focused on her Beth took a step backward. "But I didn't—"

"You did," Jared insisted, fighting his tears.

"But I didn't say she killed her, Jared. You misunderstood—"

"All right," Sam growled, cutting off her explanation. Though Merry could see he was struggling to control his temper, he guided Jared to a seat beside the reception desk and sat down beside him. "Now," he said to the boy, "I want you to calm down and tell me how all this nonsense started."

The story spilled out. Jared knew his mother had died when Sarah was born. He also knew that Merry was the doctor who'd helped his sister into the world. After asking his aunt and making sure of those points he'd put the two events together in his mind and come up with Merry as the villain.

"But son, that's just not how it was," Sam said patiently and proceeded to attempt an explanation.

Merry could easily see how the boy had become confused—*especially* if Beth had given him just enough information to send his imagination soaring. But that didn't matter now. The important thing was to set him straight.

She took a deep breath to steady her voice. "Jared, I didn't hurt your mother."

The child's eyes still held a glimmer of accusation. "But you were there."

"Merry was helping," Sam interjected. "Doctors are here to help people. You know that, Jared."

"But then why did my mother die?"

Merry slid into the seat beside the boy's. "Sometimes even though we do all we can, people still die. But it's not always the doctor's fault."

"Then why do we have doctors?"

"Because most of the time we *can* help people," Merry explained patiently. "I helped Sarah be born."

"But..." Jared began, and that word was full of doubt.

Merry decided to try another direction. "Jared, when I became a doctor I had to make a very, very big promise." She stopped, wondering how to explain an oath to a child. "It's a promise I can't break, no matter what."

"Like you swear on a stack of bibles?" he supplied.

She nodded. "I swore I would do everything I could to

help anyone who was sick. Because of that promise, I did everything I could to help your mother.''

The stack of bibles seemed to make more of an impression on him than anything his father or Merry had said thus far. The boy spent a few moments in serious contemplation.

Before he could say anything more, Beth made a belated contribution to the explanation. ''Jared, I think you just misunderstood what I said.''

And with that, Jared at last accepted the assurances of the adults. He looked at Merry with eyes as big and round as saucers. ''I guess I got it mixed up. I'm sorry.''

Daring to ruffle his hair, she blinked away some tears. ''That's okay. Sometimes I get things mixed up, too.''

''Sometimes we all do,'' Sam added and pulled Jared to him for a hug. ''But the next time you have a question about something like this, you can ask me.''

''Jared,'' Merry said. ''Did you tell Sarah what you thought about me?''

''Nah, she's such a baby, I didn't want to scare her. I just told her you were bad, and that she shouldn't like you.''

There was relief in the glance Sam and Merry exchanged. How in the world would they have explained all this to a six-year-old?

''Anyway, I don't think Sarah believes you're bad. She still likes you a lot, Merry,'' Jared said, adding a tentative, ''I guess I do too, really.''

His grin reached straight to her heart, but Merry knew better than to offend his nine-year-old sensibilities with a big display of emotion. She contented herself with a soft, ''I like both of you a lot, too.''

''So I'm not in trouble?''

His father laughed. ''You're not in trouble. Go get Sarah and we'll have some pizza.''

''And tell her Merry isn't bad,'' Sam called as the boy

scampered down the hall. Slumping back in the chair, he shook his head. "I'm sorry about all of this, Merry."

"I am, too," Beth added from across the room.

I just bet you are. Merry swallowed the angry words and was left with a bitter taste in her mouth.

"I never dreamed he'd get everything so confused," Beth continued. "He obviously misunderstood everything I said to him."

"Obviously," Sam agreed.

Merry looked at him in sharp surprise. Was he going to take up for Beth after the poison she had tried to spread?

The woman lowered her head. "And I know it hasn't helped that I've been hateful to Merry. I just don't know what's wrong with me lately." Her hand clenched over her stomach protectively. "I'm so irritable. Any little thing sets me off."

Standing quickly Sam went to her side. "You aren't feeling up to par, Beth, and we know that, but—"

"I'm sorry," Beth murmured, raising tear-filled eyes to Merry. "I'm really sorry."

Stirring uncomfortably in her seat, Merry struggled to find a reply. On one hand she wanted to accept Beth's apparently sincere apology and put the whole incident behind them. On the other hand she clung to the notion that the woman had upset Jared on purpose.

Sam took the matter into his own hands. "No one is blaming you," he told Beth. "But it would make me happy if you and Merry could get along."

"I know." Beth looked up at him, biting her lip. "I want you to be happy, Sam."

You'd think she was in love with him, Merry thought. And the idea seemed to explode in her head. *Beth in love with Sam?*

Hands clenched in her lap, she watched as he looped his arm around Beth's shoulders. The gesture wasn't uncommon. As Merry had seen at Thanksgiving, theirs was a demonstrative family. But was there something more than sisterly concern in Beth's eyes? That would explain the woman's attitude toward Merry.

As the idea took hold she sat ramrod stiff, staring at the other two and measuring their every action and reaction.

"I'm going to round up the kids," Sam said, moving toward the hall. "Why don't you two have a little talk?"

Mutely Merry watched him leave and tried to think of some plausible protest. There was none, and she was left to face Beth.

The other woman's gaze was trained on the floor. One hand was pressed to her mouth. The other was balled into a fist, still at her stomach.

My God, Merry thought, what if she really is in love with Sam? What an impossible situation that would be. And the saddest part was that Sam would never love Beth. She was Liza's sister and Bill's wife. Merry knew instinctively he would never cross that line with his sister-in-law.

Sympathy spread through her as she considered the woman's position. The emotion softened her anger, and she stood, taking a step forward with hand outstretched. "Beth," she began.

The woman looked up, and in her eyes Merry read cold, naked fear. Not the reaction she'd expected. Startled, she took another step forward. "Beth, what's wrong?"

Against her dark hair Beth's skin was white. But her brown eyes were bright, almost feverish. Her hand dropped away from her mouth. "It's just..." The eyes searched Merry's face.

"What?" Merry prompted, drawing closer.

"I'm so...afraid." The words were choked out, seemingly with great effort.

"Afraid? Of what?"

Not answering, Beth whirled around, turning her back on Merry.

"Beth?" she prompted, really concerned. "What's

wrong? You can tell me." She laid a hand on the woman's shoulder.

Beth shook it off and appeared to draw a deep breath before turning back around. The fear was gone from her eyes, but her lips still trembled. "It's nothing. I'm just being silly, that's all."

Scanning the woman's drawn, ashen features, Merry wasn't so sure. "Beth, if there's something you want to say to me, say it. That's why Sam left us in here."

"There's nothing I want to say except that I'm sorry."

The words were genuine, of that much Merry was sure. What she couldn't account for was the sheer terror she'd seen on Beth's face. "I think there's something more bothering you—"

"I said I was sorry," Beth cut in, the familiar look of dislike returning to her face.

Merry backed away. Having won the small victory of an apology, it was too much to be asking for more. "All right. Let's forget it."

"Good." The hand that Beth had clenched at her stomach moved upward, pulling the collar of her coat together. "I wonder what's keeping Sam?" she asked casually, as if all they'd been talking about was the state of the weather.

The sudden change made Merry blink in surprise and left her more puzzled than ever. "I'll go find him," she said after a slight hesitation. She headed down the hall, pausing at the corner to look back at Beth. Standing alone in the fast-darkening office, the woman looked small and somewhat forlorn.

And Merry felt there was more distance between them than ever before.

Troubled, she hurried through the clinic until she found everyone in the staff lounge, gathered around the small aquarium Amy had placed in front of the window. The children were fascinated with the tank's colorful inhabitants. Amy was patiently trying to answer all their questions.

"Everything okay?" Sam asked, coming toward Merry.

"I think so." She glanced at the children. "We'll talk about it later."

But that night when she and Sam were alone, Merry didn't know where to begin. To even suggest Beth was in love with him would invite an explosion. So Merry sat beside him on the couch, discarding first one and then another way to bring up the subject.

Like her, Sam was restless. "I think Jared's straightened out," he said finally.

"I hope so. If only Beth hadn't..." Merry paused and bit her lip.

Sam's eyes narrowed. "You don't think she got Jared so upset on purpose do you?"

"Do you?"

"Of course not."

"Then let's just forget it," Merry said, weary of the whole situation.

Sam sat up and frowned at her. "I know you're not satisfied."

"On the contrary, I'd be happy to let the entire thing drop."

But he pushed on. "What did you and Beth talk about when I left you alone?"

"She said she was sorry."

"And that's all?"

"No...." Merry hesitated and then plunged ahead. "She's very troubled about something, Sam."

"What do you mean?"

"She's frightened—"

"Frightened? Of what?"

"I have no idea, but after you left she became very upset and told me she was afraid. She wouldn't say why."

Rubbing his jaw, Sam drew a deep breath. "Aren't most pregnant women a little crazy?"

"Sometimes," Merry said slowly. In her experience, the fears of most expectant mothers was nothing like the terror she'd seen on Beth's face today.

"Liza cried a lot," Sam said.

"But was she afraid?"

He looked away, and Merry wondered if he was reliving Liza's death. She couldn't remember Sam's wife being unduly agitated when Sarah was born. Liza had been excited and eager to see her child. As Merry sorted through her own painful memories of that rainy spring night, she slipped her hand in Sam's and gave it a comforting squeeze.

His smile was grateful as he put his arm around her shoulders. "Liza was more happy than frightened."

"You'd expect Beth to be overjoyed right now, too."

"Yeah, she and Bill have been trying to start a family for years."

"And they're happily married?" Merry pressed.

Sam seemed surprised by the question. "You think not?"

"You know them better than anyone."

He shook his head, as if throwing off the notion. "No, I bet Beth's whole problem is all the changes going on in her life. There's the baby and you—"

"And why am I such a problem?"

Sam paused, carefully choosing his words. "Beth just wants me to be happy—"

"And she thinks I can't do that for you?"

"That's not exactly it."

Merry stood. "Then what?"

There was no escaping the question, but Sam remained silent. Any discussion of Beth's insecurities would of necessity mean a discussion of his own. And those were feelings he'd rather not drag out for Merry's inspection.

She didn't give up, however. "Come on, Sam. Tell me

why Beth hates me. Maybe that will explain why you keep me at arm's length, too.''

Anger curled like a hard fist in his stomach. "Have we really been at arm's length for the past few weeks?"

Merry had the grace to look a little contrite. "I guess not, but..."

"But what?" he prompted.

"But you push me away," she finished, flushing.

And instantly Sam knew she was talking about the nights they'd come so close to making love. The nights he'd held back and burned for hours after she was gone.

"I know you want me," Merry whispered, moving closer.

"It's not that simple."

"Why not?"

He ran a hand through his hair, trying to come up with the right words. "There are a lot of unresolved issues between us."

Her brows drew together in a puzzled frown. "What issues?"

He cast about for an explanation. "I don't just jump into bed with someone, Merry. That's just not my way."

"And you think I do?" Merry's eyes widened with hurt. "You're not just anyone. You know how I feel about you."

"Do I?" he countered.

"I've told you, Sam. You're the most special man I've ever known."

"The words come easy."

"So do the feelings," she insisted stubbornly.

A bitter smile twisted his lips and Merry's heart. "I want to believe you," he muttered.

"Then why don't you?" she challenged. "Is it because Beth says I can't be trusted? That I'm too different? That I'll leave?" She could see by his face that her words struck home. "Is what she says so important, Sam?"

Pain flickered across his face before he reached for

Merry. And the shudder that went through his body was so intense it shook her, too.

"Oh, Merry, it isn't Beth. It's me," he murmured in a voice full of frustration. "I have so many feelings for you. That's why I hold back. That's why I can't be casual about making love with you. Because once that happens, I know I'm never going to pull out of this with my heart in one piece."

Merry thought she started loving Sam right then. That realization had been building, of course, fueled by his strength of character, his tenderness for his children and the electricity between them. But now, when he made himself so vulnerable, her love for him began. She wondered who wouldn't love a man who could lay his feelings out like chips in a poker game. *Here's everything I have,* his words seemed to risk. *I dare you to take it away.*

Ready to gamble, she tipped her head back so she could look straight in to his eyes. Her voice was stronger than she felt. "I sure hope you don't keep your heart, Sam, because I want a part of it for myself."

"You shouldn't say things like that," he whispered before his mouth found the sensitive spot just below her ear.

She turned her head, bringing her lips to a breath away from his. "I'm not going to stop until you believe every word I say."

He kissed her with all the fire and all the passion Merry had ever wanted from a man. But more arousing than his touch were the words with which he teased her. "I'd like to believe you. I'd like to lay you right down on this floor and slide right up inside you. Right now. Right this minute." He said that, even though she knew tonight was not the night he would act on that wish.

Merry trembled with the excitement his husky voice invoked. And she knew every sensation of this moment would remain with her always. The hard muscles of his shoulders beneath her hands. The scent of smoke from the wood stove. The crazy racing of her pulse. She memorized every sigh, every caress and every breathless whisper.

That night was the beginning of a special time. A magical time, Merry thought. And with each day that passed she fell deeper and deeper in love with Sam.

Maybe the process was helped by the Christmas season. Merry considered it the first real Christmas of her life. Snow lay on the ground, a wreath decorated every door of the farmhouse, and a big, fat spruce tree stood in the corner of Sam's living room. She piled the space beneath that tree with presents for Jared and Sarah, wrapping everything separately—from the smallest box of crayons to Sarah's three-story dollhouse. Nothing, not even Beth's on-again-off-again mood shifts could dull Merry's enjoyment. Every minute Merry didn't spend at the clinic, she was with Sam and the children.

Caught in the flurry of her excitement, Sam forgot to worry about how much money she might be spending. He didn't worry about matching her extravagance. She loved the giving; he could see that on her face. She baked cookies and breads and cakes and gave them away to neighbors, co-workers and friends. They went shopping in the city, and she dropped money in every pot of every charity Santa Claus. On Christmas morning she was as excited as the children, watching eagerly as they tore into their gifts.

And because she had given so much of herself to his family, Sam decided his gift to Merry had to be worth more than mere money. While the children were playing with their new toys in the living room, Sam found a moment alone with Merry in the kitchen to present her with a clumsily wrapped package.

Expectantly he watched her hold up the silver comb and brush set that had sat on his mother's dresser for as long as he could remember.

"Sam," Merry murmured, stunned. Sarah had shown her

the set on a rainy Saturday afternoon when they'd been playing hide-and-seek upstairs. "I can't—"

He laid a finger against her lips, silencing the protest. "But I want you to have them. My mother would have liked you. She thought the only people worth knowing were those who pulled themselves up by their bootstraps and went after the things they wanted. She would have appreciated your stubbornness."

Merry smiled at the backhanded compliment and traced loving fingers across the pattern engraved on the brush. The design had eroded with time, worn away by the countless touches of other hands. Knowing the gift had been loved by someone close to Sam made the gesture all the more special.

"I don't have anything of my mother's," she whispered, still looking down. "She took everything with her when she left for good. She died in a car accident in Los Angeles right after that, and Aunt Eda Rue didn't keep anything for me."

Sam lifted her face so he could look into her eyes. "This aunt of yours wasn't very compassionate, was she?"

Merry's expression hardened, belying the nonchalance of her shrug. "I guess she tried."

"How about your aunt? Do you have anything of hers?"

"The picture over my mantel and a blue china plate that used to sit on her piano."

Watching the pain steal into her eyes, he frowned. "Where's the plate?"

"It's packed away. I broke it when I was twelve, and my aunt told me to keep it as a reminder of my carelessness."

The subtle cruelty of that made Sam catch his breath. "And you still have it?" he asked, amazed.

"Yeah, I pieced it back together, and when everything goes wrong, I get it out and look at it."

"You should throw it away."

She shook her head emphatically. "It keeps me humble."

He had no answer for that. No comfort to offer. He knew some wounds went too deep to be healed.

However, he was pleased when Merry again held up the comb and brush. "It's nice to hold a happy memory," she said, and her tone made Sam feel as if he'd given her the stars.

The day after Christmas his brother, Mike, arrived with his family for a short stay. Bill and Beth and a score of other relatives and old friends dropped by for visits, and the house was filled to overflowing.

Beth and Liza's parents, who for health reasons had moved to Arizona before their daughter's death, were among the visitors. Sam had wondered how they might react to Merry, but he was quickly reassured. They seemed to like her, especially when they saw her kindness to the children. If Beth had voiced her doubts to them, they evidently disagreed with their daughter. They told Sam it was about time he found someone with whom he could be happy.

Merry seemed to revel in the noise and the laughter. She pitched in to help with the cooking and the cleaning and hit it off especially well with Mike's wife, Nancy.

On the last night of his brother's visit Sam sat with Mike in front of the living-room fire. Friends and relatives were gone. All five of their children were finally in bed. From the kitchen came soft laughter from Merry and Nancy. A feeling of contentment had settled over the house.

"Don't let Merry get away," Mike said suddenly.

Sam turned to him, surprised. It was unlike his brother to offer unsolicited advice on anything.

"I don't want to meddle," Mike continued. "But you've been alone long enough, Sam. Don't let her go."

"You sound as if I was planning to boot her out the door."

Mike grinned. "I know you pretty well, and I've seen the way you can worry a thing to death."

Turning back to the fire, Sam felt a moment's resentment. He'd never had any of his brother's flash, had never envied Mike's quicksilver personality. It simply wasn't his style. "I don't think it hurts to be cautious."

"What will caution get you in this case?" Mike asked. He leaned forward until Sam was forced to meet his eyes. "Listen, I see the way she looks at you. Feelings like that don't just fall in to your lap everyday. So don't blow it."

His brother's advice lingered in Sam's mind over the next few days. It was the slowest time of the year on the farm, but several of Merry's patients picked the holiday week to have babies. She was at the hospital, Jared and Sarah had gone to Bill and Beth's to spend the weekend with their visiting grandparents, and on New Year's Eve Sam had plenty of time alone to think.

The long hours ticked away, marked by an inch of fresh snow and the steady approach of the New Year. Time went so fast, Sam thought. Whole days could slip away while you blinked. In so swift a world a man could lose it all by hesitating.

With that insight Sam's caution, which Merry had been straining, gave way at last. He was amazed at the ensuing calm and the subsequent flurry of preparation.

Decisions, he thought as he drove to the hospital, are best when they're finally made.

Chapter Eight

On the hospital's maternity floor Merry pushed wearily through a set of swinging doors. Three deliveries in twenty-four hours would have been normal when she was in Chicago, but her hospital visits had been few and far between since the clinic had opened. Unaccustomed to the long hours, she was worn out.

"Merry?"

She whirled around. Sam was rising from the row of chairs beside the nurses' station. Rising just as he had on the night his wife had died. As he had in Merry's nightmares. The similarity of surroundings and action was so disturbing she fell back a step.

"Merry, are you okay?"

She recovered swiftly. "What's wrong? Is Beth—"

"Nothing's wrong," he explained, taking her hands in his. "I've been waiting for you."

"But what are you doing at the hospital?"

He grinned. "It's New Year's Eve and you're my date, remember?"

Until now Merry had forgotten the party she and Sam had been invited to attend. Jeff and Amy, who had worked out their differences, were throwing a New Year's Eve gala at his place. Though Merry had promised to be there, she couldn't muster any enthusiasm for the event. "Sam, I don't think I'm up to going anywhere tonight."

"Good."

She was surprised. "I thought you wanted to go to this party?"

"Only because you did."

"But—"

Ignoring her protests and the curious looks of the nurses at the desk, he pulled her close. "I'd rather just take you home," he whispered, and the need in his voice sent ripples all the way to the pit of her stomach.

Feeling breathless, she looked up at him. His gaze was warm, full of suggestion. There was no mistaking his intentions. But Merry asked anyway. "Sam, are you saying—"

"Don't you think enough has been *said*?" Not waiting for her reply, he kissed her—a kiss that told her everything she needed to know. The nurses reacted with an approving burst of applause.

It wasn't the usually reserved Sam Bartholomew who drew away and bowed to their audience. Merry thought him very different from the man who'd been prolonging the consummation of their relationship for weeks. This Sam was obvious in his impatience. The eagerness in his eyes kindled an answering ache in her.

Her weariness disappeared as she slipped her hands back in his. "I'm through talking if you are."

"Then let's go home." He smiled, a teasing, loving smile. "You can leave, can't you?"

"Give me five minutes."

Pausing only to get her things from the doctors' lounge, Merry joined Sam outside. Snow was falling as they ran hand in hand toward his truck, and she felt as young and carefree as any sixteen-year-old. The problems with Beth, his reluctance and her own worries all faded. Laughing, she tipped back her head. The cold taste of snow was quickly replaced by the warmth of Sam's mouth. He spun her round and round across the slippery parking lot until they skidded to halt at his truck. But he kept on kissing her.

"Are we going to spend the night out here?" she finally managed to whisper.

"It's tempting."

"We might freeze."

Sam dusted the snow from her hair and let his fingers catch in the silky curls. "I think we could stay warm no matter where we were tonight."

"All right." Again her mouth tilted up to meet his.

But Sam held her back, content to gaze at her. The lights overhead were just bright enough for him to read the sweet promise in her eyes. To know that expression, even for a brief while, would be worth any risk. "You know I love you, don't you?" he murmured, becoming certain of his feelings as quickly as it took to utter the words.

She shut her eyes, and Sam knew a moment's panic. Maybe that wasn't what she wanted to hear from him. "Merry?" he prompted.

Her lashes fluttered upward, and tears trembled on their tips as she shook her head.

"What's wrong?"

"Nothing," she managed, her words tripping over each other. "I didn't know you loved me. I hoped so. I'm so happy you do."

Relieved, he stopped holding his breath but still gazed at her in concern. "If you're so happy, why are you crying?"

"Why shouldn't I cry?" Merry demanded, feeling foolishly defiant. "It isn't every day the man you love says he loves you, too."

Hidden in the words was the message Sam needed. She loved him. He could live on those words for months. Years, even. If nothing else worked out, he'd still have those words and the way she looked saying them. Tenderly he kissed her, tasting the salt of her tears as his lips skimmed across her soft cheek. Her skin was cold, at odds with the heat building inside him.

"Let's go home," he whispered again.

Home. The way he said the word sent shivers of happiness through Merry. All during the drive through the snowswept countryside, she kept repeating to herself, *I'm going home with Sam, just as if our homes were one and the same.*

Silent but cozy, the farmhouse did seem to welcome Merry. She paused in the kitchen, inhaling the familiar scents of wood smoke and evergreen. In this house there was peace, a sense of completeness she had never found anywhere else. She turned, eager to share the feeling with Sam, but her words were lost beneath his lips.

There was nothing subtle or sweet or peaceful in this kiss, Merry thought dizzily as she clung to him. He simply possessed her mouth, plundering the deepest corners with his tongue. Maybe she'd only thought he had kissed her before. And maybe those other kisses had been imitations. For never had her answering response been like this. This real. This sharp. Keen-edged and fast, her desire was a switchblade, ripping straight to her core. Was it pleasure or pain? She wasn't sure.

But she was certain she wanted more. She groaned a protest when he took his mouth away. "Sam, I want—"

"I know everything you want," he murmured, his lips against the pulse at her throat. "I can tell you every place you want to be touched. Every inch you want me to kiss. We'll get to that...." He paused, and his breath on her skin sent a vibration through her, making her breasts heavy and aching to be touched.

His name was a sigh, a shuddering sound of pleasure she couldn't stop.

Sam absorbed her shiver, adding her obvious arousal to his own burgeoning excitement. They had only kissed and already he wasn't sure where she began and he ended. This is what it's like to be lost, he thought. Completely lost in another person. As if he needed the impetus, that knowledge put new urgency in his veins.

"Merry," he said in a voice so hoarse he scarcely recognized it as his own. "I promise next time we'll take it slow. I promise you. But now..." His hands slid upward, across the heated skin of her face, tangling in her hair. "Now, I just can't wait—"

Her lips silenced him. Open, moist and inviting, they pulled him under, drowning the last of Sam's carefully laid seduction plans. And at the moment he didn't care. All that mattered was being with her. In her.

Instinct let him guide her to the couch. On the way their most unnecessary clothes scattered to the floor. His parka. Her coat. His belt. Their boots. Hasty, hurried movements filled the darkness, fueled by whispers of encouragement and sighs of pleasure.

For Sam, one sensation dissolved into the next. There was Merry's husky laughter as they tumbled onto the couch. The satin feel of her thighs as he pushed her panties and hose downward.

Later, he promised himself. Later he'd pause to savor every inch of her.

Now, however, there was no time. Her hands were working at the zipper of his jeans. His clothing was pushed out of the way. Then he was hot and heavy in her hand. He thrust forward, and her hips met him, surrounded him. Only sweet heaven on earth remained. Starbursts and roller-coaster rides and dizzying altitudes. He paused there, soaring. On the downward slide he began to wish there had been time to take her just as high.

"I'm sorry," he gasped. "I didn't plan it this way."

Merry smiled at his words and tightened her legs around his hips, holding him inside her while his breathing lost its ragged edge. What a feeling this was. Her senses were still reeling from the frenzy of their coupling, and yet she was filled with this curious calm. She had little firsthand knowledge of the emotion, but this was the way she'd always dreamed it would feel to *belong* to someone else.

Sam pushed himself up, as if to move away.

She shook her head, arms clasping him closer. "Don't move."

He collapsed into her, burying his face in her neck. "I had this all planned, you know. Clean sheets on the bed and everything."

Settling her chin against his thick, curly hair, she laughed. "I wouldn't change a thing about how this happened."

He raised up, and she could feel his searching gaze, even in the dark. "Really?"

"Yes, really. We were both about to explode—"

"But I'm the only one who did."

"Sam!" Her scandalized whisper was caught beneath his mouth. Secretly she wasn't scandalized at all. Intimate talk in the calm after the storm would only draw them closer.

Against her lips he promised, "It'll be better."

"I have no doubt."

For a few moments longer they lay silent, holding each other in the darkness. Then Sam slid reluctantly from the warm cocoon of her body.

"I wish you wouldn't," Merry protested, smoothing down her skirt as she sat up.

There was a rustle as he rearranged his clothes. "It's getting cold. Let's go to bed."

The thought of warm covers and crisp, clean sheets did

sound appealing, especially if they were to be shared with Sam. Putting her hand in his, she followed him through the quiet, dark house. Embers glowed in the living-room fireplace, doing little to chase the chill from the air. In Sam's bedroom it was downright cold, due no doubt to the curtains he'd neglected to close. Moonlight, reflected by the white blanket of snow, streamed through the windows and filled the room. The illumination was weak and dreamlike. Perfect, Merry thought.

"I'll close these," Sam said, moving toward the curtains.

She stopped him. "I like this light."

"You'll be freezing by morning."

"I'm counting on you to keep me warm."

"All right." He turned and lightly touched the curve of her cheek with his knuckles. "But I have to stoke up the fires."

He left her standing by the bed. She perched on the edge, hands nervously smoothing the uneven texture of the quilted cover. Earlier, in the sweet rush of Sam's possession, there had been no time for nerves. Now, faced with the reality of this broad bed, her tension grew. Shivering, she sat still and silent.

From the doorway, Sam spoke, causing her to jump. "Merry?" he asked in concern, coming toward her. "Are you okay?"

"I'm just being silly," she assured him. "I mean, considering what just happened between us, I shouldn't be nervous."

He settled beside her on the bed and took her hand. "But you are?"

She nodded. "Isn't it dumb? But here, in this bed—"

"This isn't Liza's bed."

She realized he had put a name to her elusive fear. *Liza.*

"I put that bed away in the attic," Sam continued. "Maybe someday when Jared or Sarah move away, they'll have a use for it."

Grateful for his sensitivity, Merry squeezed his fingers.

And Sam smiled. By putting away the bed he'd shared with Liza, he'd also tucked away some memories. They were good memories, but remembered happiness couldn't warm him the way Merry did. Sitting beside her here in the moonlight, he was more certain than ever that he had made the right decision.

"This was my grandparent's bed," he explained. "It's a little old-fashioned, but it's sturdy." He gave the curved foot rail a little shake.

"I like old things," Merry assured him.

"I figured the person who said this old house had character would appreciate this bed."

"Thank you," she whispered.

"No. *Thank you.*"

"For what?"

"For making me so happy."

She melted into his arms. "If I gave you one-tenth of what you've given me, it still wouldn't equal out."

Sam spared only a moment to wonder what he could possibly have given this beautiful, accomplished woman. The thought was swept away, however, by the passion she stirred in him. This time, he wasn't going to hurry. They had all night.

He stood and pulled her with him, turning so that they faced each other. She was gorgeous in even the brightest sunlight, but in these silver-edged shadows she was like something from a childhood fairy tale. More fantasy than fact. Only the warmth of her skin reassured him she was real.

"I do love you," he whispered, threading his fingers through hers.

"You say it like it's hard to admit."

"It has been."

"I wish I could understand why." A tiny frown puckered the skin between her eyebrows.

Leaning forward, he touched that frown with his lips, hoping to smooth it away. Failing that, he tried to explain. "I never thought I'd fall in love again, especially not with someone like you."

Not satisfied, Merry protested, "I'm just a woman, Sam."

He laughed. "That is the most incredible understatement of the year."

"But, Sam—"

He kissed her, his hands leaving hers to caress the rounded curve of her behind. With that leverage, he pulled her hard against him and settled his hips against the yielding hollow between her thighs. His voice was low and thick with need. "If you're just a woman and I'm just a man, why are we just talking again?" And he kissed her once more.

Even as she sank into the pleasure of the moment, the neat way he had sidestepped her question left Merry uneasy. Could he still have doubts about them? Even though they loved each other?

He didn't act like a man with doubts. In Sam's voice there was love. In his touch there was a gentleness, tempered with enough impatience to scatter all of her questions. He loved her. They were together in the way she had dreamed. She couldn't want anything more.

This time they undressed. Slowly. And whatever Merry had thought she knew about Sam's body was confirmed, amplified. She had felt his hard muscles, his smooth skin and the crisp furring of hair across his chest. Now she discovered the tautness of his strong legs, the sleek planes of the tight little behind she'd so often admired in his jeans.

There were other discoveries, too. Like the way he turned the simple removal of her clothes into an arousing game. Her skirt was quickly discarded. But inch by slow inch he drew her sweater upward, caressing every newly bared inch of her skin, sliding over her breasts, teasing her nipples till they strained against the lacy barrier of her bra. And when the sweater and bra were gone and she filled his hands, she felt pleasure and a tiny ballooning of pride at the firmness of the breasts pushing against his palms.

"Merry," he murmured, bending down to favor each tightened bud with the touch of his mouth, the slow dallying of his tongue.

The answering blast of heat almost rocked her off her feet.

They slipped into bed, between sheets that still carried the scents of wind and sunshine. Merry scarcely drew in the smell before Sam's nearness blocked every other sensation. Pressed flesh to flesh, the full measure of his desire was hers to savor. But still he waited, touching her, anticipating her needs. Alternately tender and demanding, his hands traced every inch of her body. His lips followed. Feather-light, they swept from the arch of her foot to the curve of her thighs. Between them. Till she tasted herself in his next kiss. Merry felt like a glass, filling to the brim and beyond....

Catching the overflow, Sam slid deep inside her. She called his name, a throaty plea that threatened to snap the fragile bonds of his control. Then he stepped off the edge, into a world of thrust and parry and tight, welcoming depths.

Merry called out again when the climax hit her. Mindless words, propelled by passion, they matched in cadence the shudders that she could feel coursing through Sam's body. For an eternity she lay beneath him, still molded to his body. As if she had always belonged there.

Drowsily, Merry realized she was using that word again—*belonging*. She belonged here. In this bed. This house. With Sam. Secure in that knowledge, she closed her eyes and floated off to sleep.

The brightness woke Sam. He woke up blinking, wishing he'd thought to close the curtains at some point during the night.

"Good morning." Merry stood in the doorway smiling. She held two mugs of what Sam hoped was coffee. Perhaps that welcome, rich aroma was the real reason he'd awakened.

"Well?" she prompted. "Aren't you going to say something? Or are you one of those people who can't talk without a shot of caffeine?"

"Are you one of those people who jumps out of bed with a smile on her face?"

"Only after a night like we just had."

Their gazes, warmed by memories, met as she came across the room. They had made love all night. Loving. Sleeping. Loving again. Sam still wondered at his stamina. But looking at Merry he didn't doubt the reason for his desire. Even wearing his old robe and thick white socks, she was a knockout. More than that, she was the woman he loved. Admitting that felt so good.

"Get in here before you freeze," he said, plumping the pillows and throwing back the covers.

Her dimple flashed as she gave him his coffee and settled by his side. "We've overslept," she murmured as she leaned against the tall headboard. "It's already eight-thirty."

"I haven't slept this late in years." Sam took a deep swallow of coffee. His sigh was grateful. "And I don't think I've ever been served coffee in bed."

"It's a decadent city custom," Merry assured him.

"I could get used to some of your decadence." His lips settled on hers, the kiss deepening so quickly her coffee was almost forgotten. Only the splash of hot liquid against his arm drew them apart in time.

Merry giggled. "You must be more careful. I don't particularly want your lap scalded, Mr. Bartholomew."

"Why is that?"

Pretending shyness, she ducked her head. "Please don't make me say."

"You can tell me," he teased, lips edging closer to hers again. She giggled once more, and more coffee sloshed. Soon, the mugs were discarded in favor of kisses.

Their ease with each other amazed Merry. She'd just spent the most passionate night of her life with this man, and now she could laugh with him, tease with him. As if being together like this was the most natural thing in the world. There'd never been this casualness with Colin. But of course with Colin she never would have been wearing a ragged-hemmed robe and drinking coffee out of mismatched mugs. Life with Colin had always been such an event. She had never felt as comfortable with him as she did at this moment with Sam.

If only she could stay here all day. What a sweet temptation that was. Duty called, however. Disentangling herself from his embrace, she sat up. "I hate to end what could be an interesting morning, Sam, but I have to go to the hospital."

"But it's New Year's Day."

"And I delivered three babies yesterday. I've got mothers to check on."

He groaned and burrowed deep into the covers. "I'll wait here for you."

With his eyes shut tight and hair tousled, Sam looked no older than Jared. And Merry had to call on every ounce of self-discipline and responsibility to keep from snuggling up next to him—patients be damned. "I have to go," she insisted. "And you have to go with me."

His eyes flew open. "Why?"

"Because you stole me away from the hospital without my car, remember?"

He groaned again, and only the threat of driving the truck by herself brought him out of bed. A shared shower slowed them down quite a bit, though, and it was nearly two hours later before Merry made it to the hospital, but glowing with happiness.

The glow lasted all day. It got her through duties at the hospital, through the drive home to pick up some clothes and all the way back to Sam's waiting arms.

They walked in the snow late that afternoon. Their boots crunched through the frozen top layer, destroying the unbroken white symmetry of the field behind the house. It was cold, with a wind that bit into Merry's cheeks. After a clear day, clouds had gathered and were turning purple and pink on the horizon where the sun had started its downward slide.

"What a gorgeous place this is." Merry pulled in a deep breath of the cold air and watched the first shadows steal across the fields.

Sam put his arm around her shoulders, nodding in agreement. "Every season has a special look. In spring the whole countryside turns green, and when we plow the fields there's a smell...it's so clean...so fresh...I can't even describe it." He grinned sheepishly. "I guess I'm a little prejudiced, but I think this is the most beautiful spot on earth—no matter what season it is."

"Did you ever want to do something else? Even just a little?"

He couldn't help wondering if she wished he had other ambitions. But he couldn't lie about loving what he did. Not even for Merry. "I guess I was born to work this farm."

"A long line of farmers." The acceptance in her voice stilled his doubts.

"Maybe the last of the line."

She looked at him in surprise. "You don't think Jared will carry on the tradition?"

"I think Jared is too smart to want to work eighteen-hour days for just enough money to pay the bills."

"Does that hurt you?"

"No." Sam paused, the gaze he'd fastened on the horizon turning thoughtful. "The teachers have been telling me since Jared was in first grade that he was exceptional. I wouldn't dare make his choices for him."

The love and pride in his voice moved Merry. "I think it's Jared's father who's the exceptional one," she whispered. "Some men think their sons have to follow right in their footsteps."

"He has to become his own person," Sam insisted, and then smiled. "And of course there's always Sarah. Maybe she'll be the farmer."

"Now that's a very enlightened thought. I'm impressed."

"Who knows what the future will bring?" he continued, drawing Merry around to face him. "Maybe the choice won't be narrowed to only Sarah and Jared."

Her gaze fell beneath the intensity in his. He was talking about children. Hers and his. A commitment was implied. A future. That should have thrilled Merry. Instead she closed her eyes against the pain it brought. It would be such a joy to have Sam's child. Such an impossible, wonderful joy.

"Merry, I'm sorry. I…" Puzzled by her stricken look, Sam drew away. Maybe he was going too fast. But last night had made him think about the future. Maybe she wasn't. Maybe just being in love was enough for her. "I'm sorry," he repeated, not knowing what else to say.

"There's no need," she said, shaking her head. "You didn't do anything wrong." She took a deep breath. "It's just that I can't have any children."

It was the last thing he'd expected to hear. "But the baby you lost—"

"Was a fluke," she completed. "Or so the specialists tell me. And even if I did conceive again, the chances are very slim that I'd carry to term."

Sam stared at her in stunned silence. He should have

realized. She'd dropped plenty of hints along the way. She'd practically come right out with it that day in the machine shed when he'd told her to stop meddling with his children and have some of her own. No wonder she had cried. He felt guilty now, knowing how he'd hurt her with those careless words.

When she spoke her voice was very small. "It doesn't make any difference to you, does it?"

"Of course not," he answered gruffly and pulled her into his arms. If possible he would have absorbed all her pain. "Why would it possibly make any difference?"

"I just thought—"

"You thought wrong." His lips brushed against her cold cheek.

Relieved, she allowed herself to sag against him. Some men might see this as an inadequacy. She should have known Sam would not.

"It must be hard to accept sometimes," he said. "I mean, considering what you do."

"I guess I'm able to separate my personal feelings fairly well. Except when some patient doesn't take care of herself. When she risks her health and her baby's. Then I get upset. I want to shake her and tell her there are so many people who would love to be in her place."

"Maybe you should follow your instincts and do just that."

"Oh, I'm tempted," Merry replied. "But for every one patient like that, there are two dozen who do all the right things. Those healthy babies are my reward."

Sam was quiet for a moment before he continued, "This explains a lot to me, you know."

"About what?"

"About you. About the way you just fell right in love with my kids."

"It was their father who was the main attraction."

The reassurance was nice. "But it doesn't bother you at all that we're a package deal, does it?"

"Not at all." She tipped her head back to look at him, brown eyes wide and loving.

He couldn't resist that look. "Then I guess I'm extremely lucky."

"I'm glad you feel that way."

Sam felt much more than that. But he didn't have the words to express how she had affected him. He could only hope to show her.

"Let's go inside," he suggested huskily. "The rest of my package is coming home tomorrow morning. I'd like to make the most of the time we have alone."

Grinning, Merry suggested a race to the house.

And once inside, their lovemaking expressed Sam's feelings. Eloquently, she thought.

Beth brought the children home early the next day. Sam had just left to do his chores, and Merry was relaxing with a second Saturday-morning cup of coffee.

With scarcely a "hello" for her, Jared and Sarah breezed through the house, full of plans for a snowman. Their aunt, however, was much slower. Sharp-eyed, her gaze lingered on the remains of the intimate breakfast Merry and Sam had shared in front of the living-room fire. Just as pointedly she glanced toward the open door to Sam's room. The rumpled bed was in clear view. Beth's disapproval was just as obvious.

Merry tried to stifle her annoyance. Since the incident at the clinic, Beth had been much more congenial. Although still moody, she'd kept her hostility less blatant. Sam thought Beth was adjusting to the idea of another woman in her sister's house, especially since her parents had seemed to like Merry. But today, with that angry look in her eyes, Merry wasn't so sure.

But she had to try to be pleasant. "Coffee?" Merry offered, attempting a smile.

"Thanks, but I'm cutting back on caffeine."

"Not a bad idea," Merry agreed. "I have most of my patients cut it out entirely."

"Really?" Beth's bland expression indicated she didn't give much weight to anything Merry might advise.

"I could get you something else," Merry offered, determined to be nice.

Two spots of angry color appeared in the woman's pale cheeks. "Thank you, but if I wanted something I'd get it myself."

The statement was an assertion of territorial rights, and Merry felt as if round three was about to start. She neither wanted nor needed the aggravation.

"Beth, I'd really like us to be friends."

"Would you? Why?"

"Why not?" Merry countered. "I'm part of Sam's life. You're part of his life."

"But we really don't have anything else in common, do we?"

"I don't think that's the point."

"I do." The words had the ring of finality to them.

But Merry wasn't giving up. She'd discarded the notion that Beth might harbor some secret crush on Sam. The idea was just too outlandish. No, there was something deeper and more disturbing behind the woman's hostility. Merry was determined to discover the source.

"Beth," she began, gesturing toward the couch. "If we could just sit down and talk, I'm sure we could work this out."

"I'm sorry, but I don't have time for a chat this morning. I have work to do at home." The voice was even, the tone light, and Beth's eyes were aimed at a spot just beyond Merry's shoulder.

Merry turned around to find Sam coming in from the kitchen.

"Hello, Beth," he said, crossing to warm himself in front of the fire. "I hope the kids didn't run you ragged."

"They were fine. You know we love to have them."

"But are you feeling okay?"

"I wish everyone would stop fussing over me," Beth protested. "I feel great." She paused. "In fact I was going to offer to do a few things around here." Her gaze shifted to Merry and hardened, but her tone was still casual. "However, it seems that *for the moment* you've got everything you need."

Merry could see Beth's subtle emphasis was lost on Sam, who was putting another log on the blaze.

"So I'll go on home," Beth finished.

"Well, be careful," he said. "And stay warm. It's cold out."

He saw Beth to the door, leaving Merry to stand in the middle of the room, shivering. She knew Beth wouldn't be happy until she and Sam were separated. If I could only understand why, Merry thought. If only...

Sam interrupted her thoughts by sneaking up behind her and slipping his arms around her waist. "Well, here we are, just you and me and the two terrors."

Soothed by his touch, Merry pushed all thought of Beth aside. "Your children are not terrors," she said.

He kissed her neck. "I'll ask you that after they track wet, muddy boots in all day long."

"If that's the worst thing they do—"

The words were no sooner out of her mouth when balls of packed snow pelted them from the side.

"Gotcha!" Jared called while Sarah giggled wildly.

Sam spun around to face his children. "Snowballs?" he sputtered. "In the house?"

In answer the two culprits let fly with two more icy missiles, both of which caught their father in the stomach. Then they dashed out to the kitchen, whooping and hollering.

"Just wait till I get hold of you!" Sam declared, charging after them. Despite the words, he was already laughing.

Merry wiped some snow from her cheek and stared after the fleeing trio. "And I wanted a family," she muttered.

Then she was laughing, snatching up her coat and gloves and running out the door. Aunt Eda Rue had always disapproved of little girls taking part in snow fights. To Merry this was the perfect opportunity to make up for some of that lost time.

Chapter Nine

Merry had always found January and February to be cold, dark months. Let down from the excitement of Christmas, she usually spent the first of the year yearning either to go back to the holidays or forward to spring. This year she changed her mind. In fact she found herself wishing life had a pause button so she could stay right in the middle of these contented months with Sam.

Time was the important element. They had hours and hours to spend with each other. Though Merry's schedule was sometimes hectic, the farm didn't make many demands on Sam in winter. They had nights in which to sit by the fire—talking, dreaming, laughing. There were weekends, too. Long walks in the frosty air. A movie and a hamburger with the kids. The Valentine surprise of an overnight stay in the city.

Even though the children made it difficult for Sam and Merry to be alone, the winter was also a time of sensual discovery. As a lover Sam was everything Merry could want. Inventive, tender, giving, he could excite her with only a look. They stole moments to be together. Late at night. On the Wednesday afternoons she had free. Once even in the truck on an obscure country road, with the heater blasting against the cold. The truck windows fogged over, and Merry was certain someone they knew was going to drive by. Perhaps the danger made it special, or perhaps every time with Sam was special. She didn't think she would ever get enough of their lovemaking.

They drew together as a family, too. Gradually, Merry's role in the children's lives changed, became more meaningful. Of course the changes made Beth resent her all the more, but Merry didn't care. If she was going to be part of Sam's life, she had to be important to Jared and Sarah.

The transition wasn't always smooth. It was one thing to be the children's friend. It was another to assume the role of a parent. Friends let you stay up late and made cookies. Parents made you go to bed and said no to an extra dish of ice cream. Balancing the best parts of each role was the only way Merry could seem to make it work.

With Sarah the balancing act wasn't too difficult. Sarah could behave like a perfect brat at the grocery store, cry when punished and still have a hug for Merry that night. Full of love and sunny of nature, she was satisfied to be loved in return.

Jared was more complex. Not that he rejected Merry. Quite the contrary. It was to Merry he came with his homework. It was with her that he shared his secret dream of building rockets and space exploration equipment. But Jared was older than Sarah—almost ten—and much more cautious by nature. And he asked difficult questions, like why Merry and his father were sharing a bed.

This last question came in March during a late Saturday supper. Merry choked on the manicotti she had prepared. Sarah looked confused. Turning pale, Sam told his son they'd discuss it later. After dinner he and Jared went out to the barn for a man-to-man talk.

Merry waited in the house, patiently helping Sarah get ready for bed. All the while, her mind was racing. They had been so careful. She didn't stay over every night. When she did, she and Sam were always up and dressed before the children came downstairs. Obviously, though, their efforts hadn't fooled Jared.

The boy looked satisfied when he followed his father into the house. He acted just the same as always to Merry, but she had to wait until both children were in bed to find out what had happened. Before answering, Sam poured himself a shot of whiskey.

"Was it that bad?" she demanded. Sam never drank anything harder than beer or wine. The bourbon was left over from his brother's visit.

He shook his head and downed the amber liquid in one swallow.

"Aren't you going to tell me what you said to him?"

Still with a dazed expression, he sat down at the kitchen table beside her. "I think Jared knows more about sex than I do."

"What did he say?"

"I started talking about it, and he said he understood it all. So I asked him to explain it to me." Again Sam shook his head. "He gave me the most detailed, scientific explanation of the process I've ever heard."

"It's nice to know sex education works in American schools."

"Yeah," Sam muttered. "That leaves it to the parents to cope with the hard part. Like explaining the reasons why people who love each other would want to do such 'yucky' stuff."

Merry grinned at his mimicry of one of Jared's favorite words. "What did you say?"

"I told him that *adults* who love each other, who are

committed to each other, make love to express how they feel. I told him the usual stuff—that when he's older, he'll know what those feelings are all about." Sam let out a deep breath. "I kept saying *adults* over and over. I just hope the conversation doesn't come back to haunt me when he's sixteen and wants the key to the car for a hot date."

Seeing the real concern in his eyes, she took his hand and tried to reassure him. "Sam, it's not as if there has been a parade of women through your bedroom."

"That's true."

"If Jared understands that making love isn't something casual, then he'll make the right choices. I don't think our being together is going to warp him. Being close to two adults who love and respect each other is a good impression for him to have to deal with."

"I think Jared understands it isn't casual. As a matter of fact, he wanted to know why we don't just get married."

Merry was stunned into speechlessness. The closest she and Sam had ever come to serious talk about the future was the day she had told him she couldn't have any children. They talked about next week, even next month, but the distant future and the possibility of marriage had yet to be discussed. Their agreement was unspoken, but she'd assumed they were building a solid base with the children before taking such a major step.

"Do you think Jared wants us to get married?" she asked hesitantly.

"He didn't exactly say that." Suddenly wishing he'd never told her that part of Jared's conversation, Sam got up and put the whiskey bottle back into the kitchen cupboard.

"Well, what did he say?"

Having gone this far, Sam had to tell the rest. But he kept his back to Merry. "Jared said that he liked you and Sarah liked you and that I must really like you and what were we waiting for?"

The blunt statement was exactly the sort of thing Merry would expect Jared to come up with. She shook her head. "It's a pity things aren't that simple, isn't it?"

The cabinet door shut with a louder bang than Sam had intended, and he stood looking down at the counter, silently agreeing with her. Nothing had been simple since she had walked into his life last September. If things were simple they would just get married and live happily ever after. If things were simple he'd know for certain that his love was enough to keep Merry happy for the rest of her life.

Why can't I get away from the uncertainties? he asked himself. Merry loved him. He believed that. And when he took their relationship one day at a time, he was filled with confidence. It was thoughts of a till-death-do-us-part kind of future that always made him hesitate. When the newness was gone from their love and their passion, would Merry be content? If asked, he knew she'd say yes. He also knew she was impetuous. Years down the road he didn't want her to have any regrets. He couldn't live with her regrets, just as he didn't think he could live without her.

"Sam?" Merry prompted.

Schooling his expression, he turned back to face her. "I guess nothing's ever simple, is it?"

His shuttered look was one Merry had seen before, and it disturbed her. They'd grown close during these last few months, but there were still times when Sam shut her out. He had fears he wouldn't share with her, and the harder she pushed the deeper he retreated into himself. Tonight, as usual, she tried and failed to draw him out. He grew quieter and quieter. But when they went to bed, he made love to her with what Merry could only call a fierceness.

Demanding and hot, his lips pushed her senses to the combustion point. "I want it to be good for you," he muttered, pulling her under his body.

She managed a breathless protest, "But it's always good, Sam."

"Then it has to be even better."

There was no time to question the desperation Merry heard in his words. There was no time for anything but responding to the rhythm of his hard, male body.

Later, while Sam slept, she slipped from the bedroom. Wrapped in his robe, she curled up on the living-room couch and used the silence to do some thinking. Sam acted as if he was trying to prove something. But what? That he was a good lover? With the way she responded to him how could he have any doubts about that? Each unanswerable question was followed by another as she sat in the darkness, hugging her knees to her chest.

Wind sent a shower of rain tapping against the windows, and Merry jumped. Rain instead of snow. Spring was on its way. Surprisingly the thought didn't warm her. Instead she shivered, the premonition of trouble raising goose bumps on her arms.

Sam appeared in the doorway, calling her name, his body draped in a blanket against the chilly air. "What are you doing in here?" he whispered, coming toward the couch.

"Listening to the rain."

He caught the sadness in her voice, and knew she'd picked up the feeling from him. The last thing he wanted was for Merry to be sad. "Come on back to bed. It's cold." She took his hand and followed him back to the bedroom.

"I wish we could go back to January and play in the snow," Merry whispered as they settled beneath the warm, homemade quilts.

He looped an arm around her waist, pulling her against him. "You'll love the spring here, too."

"I hope so."

Sam was silent, but long after Merry was asleep he lay wondering if it was her words or the rain that left him feeling so forlorn.

As it turned out, the March rain was the end to winter. Spring came early. And Sam's worries grew.

He was busy from dawn till dusk. The farm machinery had to be checked and put in top operating order. The ground had to be turned in preparation for the spring planting. As usual, he had money worries. Last year's crop had been good, but prices hadn't brought him the return he needed. He could only afford to hire one man to help him this season. His cousin Bill was in the same boat, but since Bill's place was smaller, he gave Sam a hand whenever possible.

There was little time left over for Merry. He assured her things would let up somewhat once the crop was in the ground. She told him she understood, but the doubts ate away at Sam's confidence. Now she was going to see the gritty reality of farm life. Hard work. Sweat. Small returns. He wondered how attractive he and his family would seem by the end of this season.

Merry wanted only to help Sam. At night his broad shoulders sloped with weariness. She massaged them, hoping to rub the ache away. He was tired and irritable, so she cooked dinner and saw to the children. Sam didn't want her taking over so much of the housework, but she insisted. She was at the farm more than she was at her house. Why shouldn't she do her share? He finally stopped protesting, although he still seemed unhappy about the situation. That puzzled Merry. She was glad to step in for him with the children, to do anything that would ease his burdens.

But there was nothing she could do about the columns of expenses he added and re-added with mounting frustration. She had no answers for the aging tractor or the cost of fertilizer. Most of these problems he didn't even share with her. She picked them up from conversations he had with Bill and Beth. Whether he realized it or not, Sam was shutting her out of part of his life. When confronted, he smiled with a confidence Merry could see was false. He kissed her and told her not to worry about him.

"At least he didn't tell me not to worry my *pretty little*

head," Merry murmured as she opened the window over the kitchen sink. It was Saturday afternoon on one of those late March days that feel more like the middle of May. Carried by a warm breeze, fresh scents spilled into the farmhouse. Damp earth. Budding trees. Tomorrow the weather could easily turn cold and snow could fall, but for now it was spring.

She leaned against the counter's edge and took a deep breath. Peaceful moments such as these weren't easy to come by these days. Just as Sam was busy, Merry's schedule at the clinic bordered on frantic. She still had every other Saturday free, but she had canceled her weekly afternoon off. She was also spending more and more time at the hospital.

The clinic's success had brought recognition to Merry. A group had toured the clinic last week, gathering facts for a similar setup in Kentucky. By the day's end they had offered Merry a job. The salary was impressive, as were their plans for staff and equipment. She had been flattered, but she had refused. Persistently they were still trying to woo her away.

Merry enjoyed the attention, but the offer was relatively unimportant. Though she was still dedicated to her patients, still challenged by her job, there was more than medicine in her life. Sam and the children needed her, and becoming part of this family was her first priority.

Not that it was easy. Juggling the demands of career, relationship and family was physically and mentally draining. Many days she felt unequal to the task.

Merry drew another deep breath of the sweet spring air and became aware of a new smell—the unpleasant aroma of burning food. "Oh damn," she muttered and hurried to the oven. The pineapple upside-down cake she'd promised Jared was black instead of golden brown. Another in the long line of culinary disasters Merry had been turning out in the last few weeks. Until recently, she'd prided herself on being a good cook. Grasping a potholder, she jerked the pan out and let it fall with a clatter to the top of the stove.

"Having problems?"

Whirling around, Merry found Beth coming through the kitchen doorway. The other woman wasn't smirking as Merry would have expected. In fact Beth looked healthier and happier than she had since Christmas. Her usually pale cheeks were blooming with color, and she looked pretty in a crisp yellow maternity top and blue jeans.

Despite the woman's congenial expression Merry still wasn't glad to see her. Beth was always turning up at the wrong moment and always seemed pleased to make Merry squirm. For that reason Merry forced herself to shrug off the ruined cake. "I just burned something, that's all."

"That stove's temperature setting is messed up," Beth said. "I kept asking Sam to check it. He didn't, and I finally got used to it. Maybe if *you* asked him—"

"He's much too busy to be worrying about the oven." Merry hadn't meant to sound petulant, but frustration colored her words.

Beth's mouth thinned. "Spring isn't an easy time around here," she said, her tone defensive.

"I know, and that's why I'm not going to bother Sam about unimportant details." Without ceremony Merry scraped the ruined cake into the trash can. She saw Beth wince. Merry had long since learned farm people didn't enjoy waste. Neither did she, but what else could she do with a lump of pineapple-flavored coal? "I also know how unpredictable this oven is," she continued. "I should have been paying attention instead of daydreaming at the window."

"Not much time for daydreaming this time of year, either," Beth commented, taking a seat at the table.

Merry pushed a hand through her hair, which was badly in need of a trim and a perm. Just one more thing she hadn't been able to fit in this week. "There doesn't seem to be time for much of anything," she muttered, more to herself than for Beth's benefit.

"I guess you're especially busy."

Glancing up, Merry was again surprised by Beth's absence of sarcasm. But she didn't trust that innocent expression. "The clinic is very busy," she said guardedly.

"Then it must really be hard on you—spending so much time here with Sam and the kids."

Merry gave the other woman a steady look. "I love Sam and Jared and Sarah. The time I spend here is no hardship."

Beth had folded her hands on the table. Now they fiddled nervously with the salt-and-pepper shakers. "Whether you resent it or not, being part of a farm family isn't easy. Everyone has a load to carry."

"I'm well aware of that." Merry's impatience showed in her voice. What was Beth driving at?

"I know you and Sam don't have much time for each other," Beth continued. "And no one would blame you for resenting that."

"But I don't," Merry protested.

Beth paid no attention, and on the surface her tone was casual, even friendly. "Why, even Liza used to resent the way things usually went in the spring."

Merry lowered her eyes, wondering how Beth managed to bring Liza into every conversation lately. To stifle the sharp retort that sprang to her lips, she crossed to the refrigerator. She'd get out the ingredients and try again with that cake.

"Liza used to say she barely saw Sam from March through August." Beth paused to chuckle softly. "Of course, Liza and I were raised on a farm, and we knew to expect the long hours and hard work. But still, she made it all look so easy—caring for Jared, keeping a spotless house, even helping Sam in the fields. I'm sure even Liza had her moments of frustration, though her family was her *first* priority."

The carton of eggs Merry held slipped from her grasp and splattered across the floor and against the leg of Beth's chair.

"My goodness," she murmured, looking down at the gooey mess. "This just isn't your day is it, Merry?"

Tightly Merry answered, "No, it isn't." Any hope of a good day had ended when Beth came through the door, armed with her usual barbs. It had been the same ever since Merry had taken over some of the jobs Beth used to perform for the children and Sam. No matter that Beth hadn't felt much like helping out, the woman resented Merry's intrusion into her sister's house. She never missed an opportunity to make subtle comparisons between Merry and Liza. And always Merry was left to feel inadequate, something less than the helpmate Sam deserved.

With jerky movements, Merry started to cross the kitchen and get some paper towels with which to mop up the broken eggs. She was trying to think of something to say when Sarah came running into the kitchen from upstairs.

"Aunt Beth!" the child called, quite obviously pleased to see her. But in her enthusiasm, she stepped right into the eggs, her feet flew out from under her and she slid, her head hitting the base of the refrigerator with an ominous crack.

"Sarah!" Merry and Beth reacted simultaneously. They reached the little girl at the same moment. Both of them helped haul her to her feet.

But it was Merry's arms Sarah turned to. Merry's shoulder her sobs were stifled against. Merry's gentle touch that checked her for serious injury.

Satisfied Sarah was more startled than hurt, Merry picked her up and sat down in a chair, crooning words of comfort. She didn't know who drew the most solace from the contact—herself or the child. She was new at parenting. Every bump, every fall and every scraped knee scattered her calm medical training. When Sarah's sobs had settled to a low moan and her own shaking had subsided, she looked up at Beth.

The woman was frozen in the position Merry had left her. The arms that had reached for Sarah were still outstretched, and the gaze that met Merry's was filled with hate. *Hard, crystallized hate.* In all their confrontations, Merry had never seen this unrelenting, bald emotion on Beth's face. Merry moved her mouth to say something, anything to ease the tension of the moment, but no words formed.

Beth moved, finally, and the outstretched arms folded across her swollen stomach. Then, abruptly, she was gone.

Merry listened to her rapid footsteps cross the back porch. The screen door slammed. And only Sarah's protest made Merry realize how tightly she was hugging the child.

Sam met his sister-in-law in the yard. "Hey, slow down," he said, catching her arm.

She jerked away. "I'm on my way home."

He caught her again, perplexed by the agitation on her face. "And you can't even stop to pass the time of day?"

"No, I can't."

"Beth," Sam said, "what's got you so upset?"

"You have to ask?" she flung back in his face.

"Merry?" The bright beauty of the spring day dimmed for him even before Beth gave a mirthless laugh.

"I've kept my mouth shut," Beth said in a tight, controlled voice. "I know I haven't been exactly friendly to her—"

"No, you haven't."

"But I haven't said anything to you for a long time. I've been waiting, hoping you'd come to your senses."

A tight ball of fury formed in Sam's gut. "What do you mean?"

"I mean, when are you going to realize how wrong she is? She isn't one of us. She'll always be an outsider."

"Only if you keep her that way."

Beth laughed again. "It isn't me. I'm not the problem. You're in way over your head with a woman who is never going to be satisfied with our kind of life—"

"Merry is here for me, day after day," Sam protested, trying in vain not to recognize her words as an echo of his own doubts.

"Oh yes," Beth sputtered. "Everyone knows she's practically living with you. It's the talk of the whole community. Maybe that's the way it's done where she comes from. But not around here. You know that. If you're so sure about Merry, why aren't you getting married?"

He found himself scrambling for an excuse. "The kids—"

"You think you're doing them a favor?" Tears welled in Beth's eyes. "What happens when your fancy doctor lady decides she's had it with playing house, pretending to be *Mommy*? Who's going to make Jared and Sarah understand that?"

Beth had tapped into Sam's deepest fears about the future, the fears he tried so hard to hide—even from himself. For a moment he could only stare at her.

Before he could say anything else, Beth backed away. "Why her?" she choked out. "Why did it have to be her, Sam?" With that, she stumbled across the yard, leaving him to look on helplessly as she climbed into the pickup and pulled away in a spray of gravel and dirt.

He hurried away from the truths Beth had laid out for him. Calling Merry's name, he went into the house and found her in the kitchen, placing a bag of ice on Sarah's forehead. Before he could demand to know what was happening, Merry cautioned, "Watch the floor."

He looked down at the crusty, yellowed mess and back at Merry with questioning eyes.

"I slipped and banged my head," the child supplied.

He stooped down beside her chair. "Are you okay?"

"Merry says I'll have a goose egg."

Sure enough, when Merry lifted the ice pack Sam saw the ugly, swelling bruise that darkened his daughter's forehead.

"I think it looks worse than it is," Merry told him.

"Really?" Sam straightened and gave way to the anger Beth's blunt words had built inside him. "I'd like to know just what the hell has been going on around here."

"Daddy, you said h-e-double-l!" Sarah reproached.

He ignored her, concentrating on Merry's suddenly pale, immobile face. "First Beth comes running out of the house, obviously upset—"

"I'm not arguing with you about her," she said coldly. "She has nothing to do with us."

"My family has *everything* to do with *me*," he returned.

Never having received such a look of anger from him before, Merry swallowed. She wasn't going to let this get the best of them. Beth couldn't win this easily.

Very carefully she handed the ice pack to the little girl. "Sarah, I want you to take this and go upstairs and sit quietly in your room."

"Do I—"

"Yes, you have to." Merry's voice brooked no argument, and the child left the room with only a puzzled look for the two adults.

"You should watch her tonight," Merry continued, going to the chair where her jacket and medical bag lay. "I think it's just a bruise, but she banged it pretty hard and I've never been one to fool around with any head injury."

"Where are you going to be?" Sam demanded, still angry.

"I'm going home."

And for the second time in five minutes, a woman walked out on him. He reacted with a string of curses Sarah probably wouldn't know how to spell. Then he followed Merry outside, catching her before she got into her car.

"You're not going until I find out what happened with Beth!"

"Who knows what happened?" Merry bit out. "We just had another one of our lovely little chats about my failings as your significant other. Everything else was an accident."

"What did she say?"

"Does it matter?" Wearily Merry slumped against the car. "It's never going to be any different between the two of us, Sam. Beth is always going to resent me. She'd resent anyone who tried to take Liza's place."

"That's not true. It's just that you're..." Sam stopped. He couldn't bring himself to say she was an outsider.

"I'm what?" Merry demanded. "What in the world am I doing so wrong? I try so hard." She was suddenly and completely exhausted, fed up with trying to prove herself equal to some elusive memory. Maybe Beth was right. Maybe she wasn't the woman Sam needed. Merry could accept that—if only she didn't love him, if he didn't love her.

"Tell me why it has to be so hard," she cried. "Tell me."

Sam didn't offer any answers. True, his arms closed around her. He walked her back into the house. He kissed her and said he was sorry for yelling at her. He even apologized—yet again—for Beth's hostility. He was sweet and solicitous and told her she was trying to do too much for the kids and for him.

He did everything he could to put things back to normal. But dinner was quiet, and that night the silence that stretched between them was ominous. Like the stillness of children awaiting punishment, Merry thought.

Chapter Ten

Heaving a frustrated sigh, Sam used his forearm to wipe a trickle of sweat from the side of his face. The machine shed was cool, but working on his stubborn tractor had him hot and bothered. He just didn't understand why everything had to go wrong all at once.

"Sam?" Merry called from outside.

Speaking of things gone wrong, he thought, grimacing. It had been exactly a week since the scene with Beth, and the distance between him and Merry had broadened with every passing day. Beth had stayed away, but the tension remained. Sam wasn't really surprised. The reasons for his problems with Merry were within himself, not with Beth. He just wasn't willing to examine them. Instead he buried himself in work, shying away from too much thought about the future.

"Sam," Merry called again. "Are you in here?"

With another sigh he put down his tools. "I'm back here." He turned to watch her come toward him, and as usual, he spent a moment in admiration. Merry did more for a pair of jeans and a simple sweater than any woman he'd ever known. It didn't matter that he was familiar with every curve of her body. She stirred him now the same as she'd stirred him six months ago. The only difference was that six months ago she hadn't seemed so very necessary to his happiness.

"What's wrong now?" she asked, nodding at the machine parts he'd spread over the floor.

"What do you think?" He knelt to rummage through his toolbox. "The tractor's down again. I'm trying to piece the engine together now, but who knows how long that'll last. I don't know how I'm going to make it through the summer with this damn thing."

Merry bit her lip. Sometimes she thought Sam was operating against insurmountable odds. It hurt to see him struggling so hard. If only she could do more to help. She knew even the suggestion of a loan would offend his pride. "I'm sorry," she offered finally, knowing the words were small comfort.

"Thanks." As always, he pretended to shrug off his troubles. He was never willing to share all his burdens with Merry. "I'll make it somehow," he said as he stood. His eyes rested on the medical bag she carried. "You going somewhere?"

"The hospital."

"Problems?"

"It should be a routine delivery, but I hate leaving when you're so busy and—"

"Don't worry about me," he cut in, going back to the tractor and picking up his tools.

Merry regarded his broad back with irritation. This particular view had grown increasingly familiar, and she was tired of being shut out. But now was neither the time nor the place to instigate a serious discussion. She turned to go, pausing long enough to tell him, "I've already started dinner. There's a salad in the refrigerator and a casserole ready to be put in the oven. Heat it about an hour.''

"I wish you wouldn't spend so much time cooking for me and the kids." Lately it seemed that Merry spent more time in his kitchen than he did. Sam appreciated the help, but he couldn't imagine cooking was the way she really wanted to spend her time. On those nights she came home tired from work, he wanted to tell her to stop and rest for a while. But she was always rushing around. He was always rushing around. The kids were always needing something. It was far from romantic. "Dinner is not always your responsibility," he said shortly.

Her fingers tightened painfully around the handle of her bag. It was either that or throw it at him. *What was the matter, anyway—didn't he like her cooking?* In answer, the last few weeks worth of ruined meals paraded through her brain. *Hadn't Liza or Beth ever burned a cake or undercooked a meatloaf?*

Knowing she was being petty, but irritated nonetheless, Merry had to take a deep breath to keep her voice steady. "I'm simply trying to help you out. But if you would rather I didn't—''

"I didn't say that." Sam dropped the wrench and swung round to face her. "I'm sorry. You know I appreciate your help. But you're busy, too, and I feel like I'm taking advantage of you."

His genuinely contrite words chased Merry's irritation away. "You're not taking advantage of me. You're busy, and the only way I seem to be able to help you is by fixing a few meals and helping with the kids."

"You do more than that—''

"I would if you'd let me," Merry said. "If our situations were reversed, I know you'd do everything you could for me."

"Of course I would," Sam agreed quickly. Then he paused, trying to imagine Merry dependent on him for anything that mattered. She was so self-contained, so capable of taking care of herself—physically and emotionally. From the traumas of her childhood and the heartbreak of her marriage, she seemed to have built an unshakable strength. She could handle anything. She'd never need him, at least not in the way he needed her.

She stepped close to him now, brown eyes wide and beseeching. "Sam, we have to find some time for each other. We have to talk."

"Maybe tonight."

Merry tried to smile. "That will be fine, if we're both not too exhausted." Lately it seemed they were too tired for anything—even making love. She missed the feeling of closeness, of unity. Reaching up, she gently brushed a lock of hair off his forehead.

Sam didn't mean to flinch, but he did. Only a few weeks ago even her most casual touch was the sweetest of tortures. Now the sweetness was gone. Puzzled hurt gathered in Merry's eyes, and he looked away, feeling guilty.

Her hand fell to her side, and she moved stiffly toward the door. "I guess I'll see you later, okay?"

"Yeah, later." Without another glance in her direction, he turned back to his work.

Merry kept seeing his flinch all the way to her car. She replayed his remote expression on the drive to the hospital, and it intruded throughout the hours that followed. When had this wariness sprung up between them? Only a month ago her biggest worries had been about the children. Now Sam was pulling away from her, and she didn't know why or how to stop him.

By the time she'd delivered a healthy baby boy later that night, Merry was completely depressed.

"You look like you lost the winning ticket in a lottery," Jeff Cole said as he passed her in the hallway outside delivery.

She managed a feeble grin. "I'm just tired."

"I know something guaranteed to pick up your spirits."

Only Sam could do anything about her spirits, but Jeff couldn't know that. "What have you got in mind?" Merry asked, trying to summon some interest.

"Go ask Amy."

"Amy?"

"She's down on the surgical floor gabbing with some friends. Go find her." With a smile Merry could only describe as idiotic, Jeff disappeared through the delivery-room doors.

Curiosity aroused, Merry found her nurse surrounded by a group of giggling, white-uniformed women. "Jeff said for me to find you," she said.

Amy extended her left hand. A diamond glittered under the hall lights. Nonplussed, Merry stared first at the ring and then at Amy's animated face.

"Aren't you going to say anything?" the grinning brunette demanded.

"Oh, Amy," was all Merry managed before her friend grabbed her in the most exuberant of hugs.

"Merry, I'm so happy."

They laughed and cried and hugged for several more minutes, but Merry couldn't get the whole story because of the many interruptions. Amy had worked at the hospital before being hired by the clinic, and she had plenty of friends still on staff. News of her engagement had spread through the hospital grapevine, and everyone on duty this Saturday night wanted to congratulate her. Finally she and Merry retreated to a corner of the cafeteria for coffee and a chat.

"I'm surprised you're not rushing back to Sam's," Amy said as they took a seat. "That's where you're always headed these days."

Merry sighed. "Quite honestly I'd rather stay here and celebrate your happiness."

"Uh-oh. Sounds like trouble. What's—"

"We're not talking about me," Merry interrupted sternly. "I want to hear all about how that ring ended up on your finger."

Amy's green eyes softened as she explained how Jeff had gone down on bended knee earlier that evening to ask for her hand in marriage. "Except for Jeff getting called to the hospital, it was all very romantic, exactly the way I've always dreamed the right proposal would be."

"You're sure this is the right proposal?" Merry teased, knowing Amy's history of broken engagements.

"One hundred percent positive," Amy said, gazing down at her ring. "I think I've been in love with Jeff for years. But first he was getting a divorce, then he went back with his wife and I felt betrayed, and—"

"But how did this all come about? I mean, I knew you and Jeff had worked out your differences, but I didn't know you had progressed to this."

Amy stirred some creamer into her coffee and shot Merry a sly glance. "Well, you've been pretty wrapped up in your own serious relationship."

"Maybe too wrapped up," Merry said glumly.

Instantly her friend leaned forward, concern in her eyes. "What's wrong, Merry? You and Sam are together all the time. I thought you'd have a ring before I did. In fact, I figured you'd skip that step altogether and just go get married."

"I can assure you that Sam would never do anything so impetuous."

"But you would."

"It's not my decision alone."

"What's the problem?" Amy pressed. "It's not that neurotic sister-in-law of his, is it?" Merry had told her friend about Beth's interference and hostility. "If Sam had any gumption, he'd tell her to take a hike."

"Tell his wife's sister to take a hike?" Merry raised an eyebrow.

"His wife is dead," Amy stated bluntly. "You're very much alive and very much in love with him. And it's obvious he's in love with you. I don't understand his dilemma."

Merry took a sip of her lukewarm coffee and turned her gaze to the nearly deserted cafeteria. After a moment's hesitation she gave voice to her deepest fear. "Maybe I'm not the sort of woman he wants as a permanent part of his life."

Leaning back in her chair, Amy frowned. "That's ridiculous. You told me from the beginning he wasn't the kind of man who goes for a casual fling. If he's not serious, what have you two been doing for the past few months?"

"I don't know." Merry had to swallow the lump that rose in her throat. "I've tried so hard, Amy. I've tried to be there for the children and for Sam. It hasn't been easy with how busy we've been at the clinic, but I've done everything I could to meet everyone's needs and become part of their lives."

"Maybe you've tried too hard," Amy suggested. "You can't be superwoman, Merry. No person can play all the roles. Surely Sam doesn't expect that of you."

Merry shook her head. "Obviously I haven't done enough, because Sam and I aren't any closer to a real commitment."

"I wonder what he'd do if he thought he was going to lose you?"

"What do you mean?" Merry asked, glancing sharply at her companion.

"Nothing. I was just thinking out loud." Her expression blank, Amy swallowed the last of her coffee. "Maybe what you two need is an evening out. Come to dinner at my place tomorrow night and help Jeff and me celebrate."

Merry hesitated.

"You need it," Amy prodded. "And I know Sam won't have worked himself to death on a Sunday."

"Let me call you in the morning," Merry said. The

thought of an evening with Jeff and Amy was tempting. Maybe it would give her and Sam some perspective on their own problems—whatever those problems really are, she added to herself.

She asked Sam about it later that night, and he seemed eager for an evening out, too. His reasons, however, were different from Merry's. "I know you're sick and tired of spending every night at home," he said, looking up from the farm accounts he'd been poring over.

That wasn't what Merry wanted to hear, and she gave in to the desire to vent her frustration. "I'd rather you wanted to go for yourself. Because you like Amy and Jeff. Because you want a break from the usual grind."

"I said I wanted to go. Isn't that enough?" Sam demanded impatiently.

It wasn't, but Merry didn't want an argument. Grabbing up a book she'd been too busy to read, she went to bed. Sam didn't join her until sometime early in the morning. Troubled and unhappy, Merry wished she had gone to her own house to spend the night.

He was apologetic the next morning, as was she. Calling an unspoken truce, they spent the afternoon with the children. The day was windy and cool, perfect for flying kites. Sam and Jared sent their colorful contraptions soaring. The kites hovered, seemingly indestructible, in the clear April-blue sky.

Imaginative as always, Sarah concocted an elaborate story for why the kites could fly so high and so long. "It's fairy wings," she told Merry. "The field fairies are really flying the kites. Not Daddy and Jared."

Merry had read *Thumbelina* to Sarah a few nights before, so she knew where the fairy ideas were coming from. Sitting on the old blanket they had spread on the ground, she listened fondly to the little girl's fanciful tale and watched the kites float in the wind. Merry thought they were a little like her hopes—strong in the right breeze, fragile if handled the wrong way. And she wondered if Sam knew how many of her dreams he controlled, as surely as he held the strings of his kite.

The kites finally, inevitably, crashed to the ground, causing Sarah to burst into tears.

Sam undertook an elaborate explanation for their fall, but Merry simply gave the child a hug. She knew logic had little do with fairy wings or even well-cherished hopes and dreams. Logic was no comfort when everything comes crashing down.

Merry's thoughts made her melancholy, a feeling that lingered as she and Sam drove to Amy's apartment that evening. Amy had prepared a real celebration, making her small dining room elegant with fresh flowers and the mellow glow of candlelight. Jeff was at his teasing best, and Merry found it impossible not to respond to the relaxed, happy mood. Even Sam unwound and seemed to enjoy himself.

Amy had just served coffee and dessert when she dropped her bombshell. "Merry, what are you going to do about that job offer in Kentucky? I heard they called you again on Friday."

Immediately Merry's gaze flew to Sam. With a bite of cheesecake halfway to his mouth, he paused and then placed his fork on his plate. His blue eyes seemed to harden.

Amy's look flashed between them. "I'm sorry, hadn't you told Sam about it yet?"

"No, I hadn't," Merry returned evenly.

"I'm sorry." There was genuine guilt in Amy's voice. "Me and my big mouth. Just forget—"

"I didn't know anything about it, either," Jeff interrupted, seemingly oblivious to the tension surrounding him. "What's going on, Merry? Someone trying to steal you away from us?"

Sam almost winced at the man's choice of words.

Numbly he listened while Merry explained the job she'd been offered. A huge new facility in a coal-mining district of Kentucky. At least four doctors under her supervision. A chance to help many more needy people. A perfect opportunity for someone as talented and dedicated as Merry. He knew she loved her work now, but ever since Christmas she'd been fretting because there was no money for another doctor and new equipment. This job would give her everything she wanted. A feeling heavy as concrete settled in Sam's gut as she talked.

"So what do you think?" Jeff asked Merry.

"I don't think she's had time to think about it," Amy put in, her smile nervous.

"I don't need to think about it," Merry said firmly. "I'm very happy right where I am. I wouldn't consider leaving the clinic or—" she paused, her gaze fastening once more on Sam "—or anything."

Everyone's gaze shifted to Sam, and a moment of awkward silence followed. He tried to think of something to say, something witty and quick that would make them all laugh. He couldn't, though. All he could think was that Merry was giving up a career move to stay with him. A part of him was filled with happiness. The other part... Well, he didn't want to explore his other, uneasy feelings.

Amy finally filled the uncomfortable pause, shifting the conversation to some harmless gossip. Merry didn't say anything. She was too puzzled by Sam's reaction.

Maybe she should have told him about the job offer, but it hadn't seemed important. She was happy with the job she had, and she was in love with him; she didn't want to leave. But he didn't seem too thrilled with that news. If he loved her, why wasn't he happy?

Before the evening was over Amy pulled her into the kitchen. "I'm sorry, Merry. I really thought Sam knew about the job offer."

"It's okay."

"No, it isn't," the brunette insisted, her expression miserable. "I saw the looks on your faces. I was just going to tease him a little about the job, maybe make him see he could lose you if he didn't get off his duff."

Merry shook her head. "I told you before, Amy. He's not the kind of man you can play games with."

"I just hope I didn't make him angry."

"Why should he be angry?" Merry replied, becoming irritated herself. "I'm not even considering that job." She stopped as a new thought occurred to her, a thought that made her throat tighten with fear. "Maybe that's the problem," she whispered.

Amy frowned. "What are you talking about?"

"Maybe Sam wants me to leave."

"Don't be ridiculous."

But Merry couldn't shake the cold feeling of dread. "With the way he's been acting lately I'd believe anything."

"Then talk to him. Find out what he's thinking."

The advice was good. Merry knew the only way to solve the problem was to communicate, but that was easier in theory than in practice. Sam was a master at hiding his feelings. She tried, however, on the way home.

"I'm sorry I hadn't mentioned the job offer—"

"That's okay," he said quickly. Too quickly, Merry thought. "We've both been busy. You said you wanted to talk last night and we never got around to it."

"This stupid job wasn't what I wanted to talk about," Merry muttered, almost to herself.

Sam heard her, and though he could have kicked himself for pursuing the subject, he said, "It doesn't sound like a stupid job at all. In fact I'd say it has a lot going for it."

"But it's in Kentucky," Merry added, pushing back the fear his words aroused. "Where I don't want to be."

There was no response from Sam.

She glanced across the darkened car, trying to catch a

glimpse of his expression. But they had left the lights of town behind, and the only illumination was the dim glow from the dashboard. It was impossible to see his eyes or even guess what he might be thinking. If only he would give her some kind of reassurance, Merry thought, biting her lips.

Finally when the silence pressed too heavily at her, she reached out and touched his arm. He didn't flinch away this time, but he didn't say anything, either. He didn't make a move to take her hand in his. The only sounds were the rumble of the truck's engine and the low, mournful strains of a country song on the radio.

So Merry forced herself to put her fears into words. "Do you think I should consider this job?"

Why is she asking me? Sam thought. *If she really doesn't want the job, why does she keep bringing it up?*

The gears ground as he turned the truck into his driveway, and he drew it to a halt at the back of the house before he replied, "I think you have to make decisions about your career all by yourself." He punctuated his sentence with the slam of his door.

Merry sat ramrod stiff in her seat, letting the anger spread through her veins. *He's not going to do it,* she told herself. *He's not going to take what we've meant to each other and throw it in my face. Not without some damn good explanations.*

Slamming her own door, she followed him to the house, ready for battle. The sight of the children in the kitchen stopped her.

"What are you still doing up?" Sam demanded of Jared.

The teenaged neighbor he'd hired to baby-sit answered for the boy. "They just wouldn't go to bed, Mr. Bartholomew. I'm sorry."

"Not as sorry as they're going to be," he snapped, his angry gaze on the children. "Get in bed. Now!"

Sarah's lower lip trembled, and Merry recognized the

first signs of a tantrum. It was always this way on Sunday night when the children resisted the return to a regular routine. After weeks—months—of practice, she knew how to get them settled. The impatience she could see on Sam's face wasn't the right method. She reined in her own temper.

"I'll get them in bed," she said, taking Sarah's hand while she nodded at the baby-sitter. "Why don't you take Linda home, Sam?"

Running a hand through his hair, Sam gave a shrug of agreement. He headed outside, leaving the wide-eyed teenager to follow him to the truck.

Under Merry's firm instructions, the children filed up to bed. Jared's eyelids were drooping before she even kissed him good-night. Sarah was more difficult, demanding to hear a chapter of her latest storybook. Even then she resisted sleep. In the dim light of the bedside lamp, Merry sat stroking the thick chestnut hair that was so like Sam's in color and texture.

"I don't like baby-sitters," Sarah announced.

Merry smiled. She had hated baby-sitters, too. "Oh, I bet Linda was pretty nice. Didn't she play games with you?"

"Yes, but I'm not a *baby*. Why couldn't Aunt Beth stay with us?"

Considering her words carefully, Merry said, "Aunt Beth's baby is getting ready to be born in about a month, and she needs to rest." That was the explanation she'd been giving for Beth's absence all week long.

"Jared says it's because you don't like Aunt Beth."

And Jared sees and understands way too much, Merry thought. She endeavored to explain. "Your aunt and I don't always get along, but I don't dislike her, Sarah. Someday I hope she'll be my friend. Maybe after she's had her baby and she's feeling better—"

"Do babies always make you sick?"

Merry laughed and leaned down to kiss Sarah's smooth

cheek. "No, sweetheart, babies are very special. Most of the time they make people really happy."

Yawning, Sarah turned on her side. "You won't forget tomorrow night, will you, Merry?"

"Tomorrow night?"

Instantly the child was wide awake again. "The dinner at school. I told you about it last week." There was a trace of panic in her voice. "You can still come, can't you?"

"Of course I can," Merry soothed. The dinner was a mother-daughter affair the school held every year for the first-graders. That Sarah had asked her meant a lot to Merry. But in the tension of this week with Sam, she had forgotten it.

"Please don't forget," Sarah pleaded. "I told everyone in my class that I was going to bring a doctor who is almost like my mommy."

Almost like my mommy. The words warmed Merry beyond measure, but still she had to caution Sarah. "Now remember, I told you that only one thing could keep me from coming to that dinner."

"E-mer-gencies," the little girl enunciated.

"You understand, don't you?"

"Yes, but I don't want any 'mergencies tomorrow night."

From the doorway, Sam spoke, causing Merry and Sarah to jump. "If a certain little girl I know doesn't get to sleep, she's not going to be able to stay awake for any dinner tomorrow night." He came to stand beside the bed.

Sarah giggled. "You scared us, Daddy."

Leaning across Merry, Sam gave his daughter a kiss. "Go to sleep."

"All right." Sarah's eyes shut again.

Intensely aware of Sam's nearness, Merry eased up from the bed and switched off the lamp. They stood, side by side in the dark, looking down at Sarah. And suddenly the anger Merry had felt toward him earlier returned in full measure.

Just as their coming together had affected this child, so would their parting. How could Sam even think of ruining what they had already built?

She turned on her heel and left the room. Sam followed her downstairs where she confronted him. "All right, I want to know what's going on with you."

"I don't know what you mean," he answered mildly as he opened the refrigerator and took out a carton of milk.

"Don't give me that stoic look."

He raised an eyebrow. "Stoic?"

"Totally indifferent. You don't look at me, you look through me."

"I didn't know I could do that."

Angry tears gathered behind her eyes, and she blinked to clear them. *She wasn't going to cry.* "I want a straight answer to what I asked before. Do you want me to take that job in Kentucky?"

"I gave you an answer. That decision is up to you."

She couldn't argue with that look. Or that cold, implacable voice. In fact, she couldn't stand to see or hear him anymore tonight. So she left.

And this time Sam didn't go after her. Gripping the cold milk carton, he just listened to her leave. Couldn't she understand? he thought. Accepting or rejecting this job *was* her decision. If, as she said, she wanted to stay, then he thanked God. But he couldn't do anything to affect that decision. At some point in the future he didn't want Merry to be able to say he had held her back. Staying had to be her choice.

Deep inside him, a tiny voice suggested his silence might be driving her away. As always Sam ignored it. Smothering an oath, he put the milk back in the refrigerator. He pulled off his coat and tie and got out the farm accounts. Maybe these problems would keep his mind off all his other dilemmas. At this moment he'd rather do anything than think about Merry.

* * *

After a nearly sleepless night, Merry woke with a nagging headache. It persisted and deepened, despite the medication she took all day. Every time she thought about Sam the pain just got worse.

The full slate of patients didn't help. Neither did the emergency C-section Merry was forced to perform late in the afternoon. The baby was breech. The mother was only seventeen. And for a few tense moments in delivery, Merry was certain she'd lost them both. As one of the assisting nurses put it, only a miracle saved them.

Exhausted, it was only after Merry had checked the mother for one last time that she realized the time. It was eight o'clock and she had missed Sarah's special dinner.

Leaving instructions to be called if anything changed with her patient, Merry flew out of the hospital. Her car ate up the miles to the farm while she prayed silently that Sarah would remember she had been warned about emergencies.

"If only I'd called," she whispered guiltily.

At the farm the sight of Beth's pickup in the driveway made Merry groan. The woman's disapproval was all she needed tonight. Squaring her shoulders, she headed for the house.

Just like the night before, Sarah met her at the door. "You forgot," she accused.

Merry dropped to her knees in front of the child. "Oh, Sarah, I had one of those emergencies I told you about."

"Why didn't you call?"

"I just got so busy, sweetheart, and the lady who was having the baby really needed me." Merry watched a little of the disappointment slip away from the child's face as she continued, "I'm so sorry. I wanted to be at your dinner so much. Did you go anyway? Did your Daddy take you?"

"No. I did." Beth rose from the kitchen table, a smug look on her face. "When you didn't show up, Sam called me."

"Well, I'm glad you were able to take my place," Merry

managed to say gracefully as she got to her feet. "I appreciate it. I didn't want Sarah disappointed."

"Really? Then why didn't you call and say you couldn't make it?"

Merry took a deep, calming breath and mentally counted to ten. She was determined that Beth wouldn't upset her tonight. "I already explained that. I had an emergency—"

"That was more important than Sarah?"

"Important in a different way."

"Explain that to her."

Looking down, Merry was reminded that Sarah was still in the room, taking in every word that was said. Jared, too, had come to stand in the doorway from the living room. "Beth, I think we can talk about this later."

"Why? So you'll have a little time to think up some sugar-sweet excuse?"

Merry felt color suffuse her cheeks. "I don't have to make excuses to you."

"I'm not asking for excuses for myself. Just explain to Sarah why you weren't here. And to Jared. And to Sam." Beth sniffed. "Seems to me you're going to be needing lots of excuses if you stick around here."

"What do you mean?"

"I mean, having a family will interfere with the rest of your life, Dr. Conrad. I imagine you'll be disappointing people a lot."

Merry took a step forward, clenching her fists. "You have no right to talk about anyone being a disappointment, Beth. You've certainly disappointed Sam during these last few months. When he met someone he could love, when he didn't have to be alone anymore, you couldn't even give him your support—"

"I'm not going to support a losing cause."

"You see! You've done nothing but try to tear us apart. You don't want Sam to be happy, to have anyone to share his responsibilities with. Why is that?"

"If I thought you *could* handle those responsibilities, I might feel differently," Beth retorted.

"I can—"

"Oh, really? Then explain tonight to me. Is that how you handle promises to little girls?"

"Aunt Beth," Sarah interrupted, "Merry told me about 'mergencies—"

Ignoring her, Beth kept badgering Merry. "What makes you think you can ever take my sister's place?"

The question caused Merry to falter for a moment. She knew she couldn't take Liza's place. Maybe that was the real problem between her and Sam. He needed another Liza, and she just didn't fit the bill.

"You can't do it," Beth said, a victorious smile twisting her mouth. "You can't ever be what Sam needs."

"That's not for you to say—"

Sam stood on the porch, rooted to the spot by the harsh, angry voices that spilled out the open windows. He didn't agree with all that Beth was saying, but as usual her words were underscoring the essential differences between him and Merry. He was a simple man—simple wants, simple job, simple life-style. From her job to her background to the way she looked, Merry was anything but simple. Trying to fit their lives together was like working on a jigsaw puzzle in which all the pieces were the same color. Frustrating. Maybe impossible.

At least Sam thought so. Standing here, dog-tired from work and exhausted by the battle raging in the house, he wasn't a hundred percent sure of anything. Except that he needed some time to sort out his feelings—without Merry or Beth to influence him either way. To that end, he went inside.

He had to shout to make himself heard. "What is going on?"

Both women wheeled around and stared at him, but neither spoke. Beth paled and sat down heavily in a chair. Merry stood her ground, cheeks flaming.

Noting the wide-eyed, frightened looks of the children, Sam told them to go upstairs. For once he got no arguments. When they were gone, he turned back to the women. "Was it necessary to have this argument in front of them?"

"I'm sorry—" Beth began lamely.

"You should be," Sam bit out. "If you're quite through, why don't you go? I'd like to talk to Merry."

Beth stood and moved toward the door, but the look she sent toward Merry was still full of hate. "I am sorry for upsetting the kids, Sam, but I'm not sorry for what I said to Merry. There's been nothing but trouble since she—"

"Me? Trouble?" Merry's words tumbled out with a bitter laugh. "You're the trouble."

"Dammit, could you both just let it rest?" Sam demanded.

Both women were silent, and with a last scathing glance, Beth left Merry and Sam alone.

"I wish she would stay out of it," Merry said, closing her eyes.

"She thinks she's right," Sam said. "She doesn't think we belong together."

Unbelieving, Merry gaped at Sam. She didn't know why he always defended Beth. "Does what she think matter so much to you?" she asked, trying hard to keep her voice steady.

Not answering, Sam rubbed a hand over his face. Damn, but he was tired, so tired he could barely put two thoughts together. All he really wanted was to be alone. "You and I need some time apart, Merry."

Something within Merry started to crumble.

"I want some time to think," Sam continued.

"About what?" she whispered.

"About us and where we're going and if we're going to get there."

"Don't you think I have a right to be in on decisions like that?"

Her brown eyes were big and full of hurt. Sam couldn't stand seeing that look. He turned away. "I can't think when you're here all the time, Merry. I have so much on me with the kids, the farm—"

"It all might seem easier if you'd really share some of those burdens with me, talk to me about them," Merry returned. Catching his arm, she pulled him around to face her. She wasn't going to let him shut her out. Not this time. "Is that it, Sam? Have I not done enough to help you? Are you worried that I—"

He cut her off by shaking his head. "I just have some things to think through."

Those words sounded like an excuse to Merry. A kind way of letting her down easy, of telling her he didn't want her in his life. "I thought you loved me," she accused, her voice thick with the bitterness of betrayal.

"I do." Sam put every ounce of love he possessed into those two words. This wasn't a matter of love.

But Merry didn't understand. "You couldn't love me. If you did, you wouldn't send me away."

"I just can't be with you right now, Merry."

Her tears overflowed. "Boy, I've heard that one before. Mother always said that before she went away, when I was begging her to take me with her."

The pain in her voice almost shredded Sam's resolve. "Merry," he murmured, stepping forward. "I'm not sending you away for good. I just need some time—that's all I'm saying."

"I think what you're really saying is goodbye." Merry backed toward the door, the hurt and anger at war inside her.

"But I'm not," Sam protested. "I do love you—"

But she was gone, leaving his words to echo in the stillness.

Chapter Eleven

The time Sam wanted to himself was in plentiful supply during the next few days. He spent long hours in the field, his solitude broken only by the steady drone of the tractor or the occasional questions of his hired hand. Hard work had always been his sanctuary, and he didn't abandon it now.

An April freeze moved in, and he shivered in the cold wind. But by Friday afternoon it was warm and humid, with storm clouds on the horizon. His thoughts were as unsettled as the weather.

Watching his plow bite through the dark, loamy soil, Sam replayed the last few months with Merry. She had changed the entire focus of his life. And no matter what happened he would never live in the same narrow little world. Before she appeared in his front yard last September, there had been his farm and his children—period, end of story. At the edges had been Beth and Bill and the assorted other family members and neighbors, but Sam's days had been long and hard and lonely. With Merry the days might still be long and hard, but there was a light at the end. And even without Merry he knew he was changed forever.

Right now he could hear her laughter. See her warm, dark eyes. Her silky auburn curls. Sam knew he could live the rest of his days and never forget the smallest details of how she sounded, looked, felt. Even now he could hear the breathless little sound she made at the height of passion. He could feel the touch of her hands, taste the honey-sweetness of her mouth as it opened under his.

With a start he realized his tractor had drifted to a halt and was idling in the middle of a half-plowed field. He shook his head and put it in gear. He couldn't lose himself in memories. He had the future to think about.

A part of Sam wished he could be impetuous. To heck with what the future might hold, he wanted to say, I'm taking what's here and now. If he could get past those worries about tomorrow, he'd sweep Merry away, marry her and dare anything to tear them apart. Ever since the night they'd had dinner in the city, Sam had been following the impetuous path, living day by day. But that behavior was wildly out of character. And now, finally, his normal cautiousness had taken over again.

Caution had sent Merry away. Caution had him back in the lonely cycle of long days and even longer nights. Caution had him miserable.

His brother had warned him, Sam remembered. Mike had told him not to lose Merry by worrying about tomorrow.

"Fine advice from someone who wouldn't be around to pick up the pieces," he muttered.

For Sam was very certain what he had with Merry would shatter. If not now, then next month or next year or years down the line. She might love him today, but there'd come a time when she would realize her mistake. For all her fine talk of family, he was sure, as he had been from the start, that someday she'd want something more than he had to give. And where would that leave him?

It boiled down to two choices, he decided. He could follow an impulse and live each day as it came, waiting for heartbreak. Or the break could come now—he could take his memories and go forward. Alone. And maybe that was the best choice of all. A clean, uncomplicated break.

Following the first choice would require Merry's cooperation, anyway. Remembering the wounded look in her eyes on Monday night, Sam wasn't entirely sure she'd be willing. He had hurt her. Maybe she was already planning to take the job in Kentucky. But he couldn't imagine she'd leave without at least saying goodbye to the children.

Jared and Sarah were part of the picture, Sam thought. Their needs had to be considered, the same as his. Trouble was, he knew what they wanted. Merry. They'd been full of questions during the last few days: Where was Merry? Why hadn't she called? Was she mad at them?

Sam put them off. Until he sorted out his own feelings, he couldn't tell them anything. But he did give them strict instructions that Merry wasn't to be called or bothered. They didn't understand. They missed her. As did he. God, how he missed her. The big old house she had professed to love held a peculiar emptiness these days. He didn't know how he was going to get used to that emptiness again.

He turned another corner in the field, and, as if conjured up by his thoughts, he saw the children running toward him. Having shot up an inch since Christmas, Sarah was doing better at keeping pace with Jared. Her seventh birthday was in two weeks. Seven years since Liza had died, Sam realized with a start. Liza's death used to be the benchmark by which he measured all time—everything fell before that night or after. But it had been months since he'd looked at his life that way.

What comes next? he asked himself suddenly. *Before and after Merry?* Yes, that was exactly how he would be dividing his life from now on. But did he really want the "after" part to be without Merry?

Not daring to answer his own question, he drew to a halt as the children came abreast of the tractor. "What are you two doing?"

"Aunt Beth sent us out to see what you wanted for dinner," Jared called over the noise of the engine.

"Aunt Beth?" Sam hadn't seen or talked with Beth since Monday night. He didn't know what he'd say to her when he did. Though he had been the one to ask Merry to leave, he didn't appreciate Beth's interference.

"Yeah," Jared said. "She was washing dishes when we got home from school."

Sarah wrinkled her nose. "She said we were slobs."

"We told her Merry hadn't been out to see us this week," Jared added.

Sam glanced sharply at his son. Just how much had Jared figured out about this whole situation, anyway? Of course it wouldn't take an overly bright child to realize there was something wrong between Merry and Beth, especially since that scene the other night. And Jared was more perceptive than most.

"Come on up," Sam invited the kids. "I'm almost finished for the day. I'll ride you back."

Beth met them at the kitchen door. In her eyes was no trace of guilt or remorse. She acted just as she would have months ago. "I thought you were coming right back to tell me what your father wanted for supper," she admonished the children.

"Merry and Daddy always made hamburgers on Fridays," Sarah said, heading for the refrigerator.

"With French fries," Jared added as he hopped up on the counter to retrieve some glasses from the cabinet. "And ice cream for dessert."

As the kids poured some juice and went into the living room, Sam saw Beth's eyes narrow with annoyance. Too bad, he thought. If she didn't want to be reminded of Merry she'd come to the wrong house.

"You don't have to cook our dinner," he told her. "What's Bill doing?"

"I thought he could come over here. You know, just like old times."

Obviously Beth thought Merry was gone for good and things could return to normal. Sam almost laughed. What was normal anyway? He didn't want a return to those pre-Merry days. Acknowledging that made him pause.

Blithely Beth continued, "It's been too long since the whole family had an evening together."

An evening without Merry is what she really means, Sam thought, feeling a tug of impatience. But to him and the kids Merry had become part of the family. He checked his temper, however. Arguing with Beth wouldn't help matters. "I'm not very good company," he warned her mildly, hoping she'd take the hint and leave.

She hesitated a moment, pressing a hand to her rounded stomach. Only a month away from her due date, she was half the size Liza had been with Jared or Sarah. "Listen," she said in a low voice, "I know this thing with Merry hasn't been easy, but in the long run you'll see it's all for the best."

Her assumption that Merry was gone really irritated Sam. He knew Beth's heart was in the right place, but she didn't run his life. She was family. He loved her and was grateful for all the things she'd done for him and his children. But love and gratitude gave her no right to act as she had toward Merry. And he wasn't going to let her think she had scored a victory.

"What's all for the best?" he asked casually, pouring himself some juice, too.

Beth's self-assured expression slipped a little. "That Merry is gone, of course."

"Is she?"

"Well," Beth sputtered, "I thought she was. The kids said—"

"The kids don't know anything about Merry and me."

"But—"

"And neither do you."

As expected, Beth's puzzlement turned to anger. Sam ignored her. He went to remind Jared of his evening chores and left his sister-in-law fuming in the kitchen. Telling her off was something he should have done months ago.

Wait till I tell Merry, he thought before he could catch himself. He might not have the chance to tell Merry anything. Not even goodbye. Could he really let her go?

As he emerged from the house and into the warm spring air again, Sam heard the rumble of distant thunder. The clouds on the horizon were darker, more threatening than before. The smell of rain was as sharp, as well-defined as the regret that settled in his gut. He knew with growing certainty that he would carry this regret forever if he lost Merry. He would spend the rest of his days wondering if they could have made it work.

And why? he asked himself. What had made him so certain it *wouldn't* work? Merry had done everything in her power to prove how much she loved him and his children. And he loved her, too. God, how he loved her. For months now, they had made each other happy. Were those months just an illusion? No. Of course not.

As for Merry not being content with farm life—well, she'd been pretty content so far. She had seen the hard work. She knew he wasn't rich. She had to know farming was the only kind of life he wanted. She hadn't run away from those cold hard facts. Sam had let his own fears blind him to what Merry had told him all along—she could accept him just the way he was.

The first hard drops of rain stung Sam's cheeks as he sprinted toward the nearest barn. While the downpour started outside, he laughed, feeling suddenly free. He was tempted to head for town right now, to talk things through with Merry. But his caution still ruled. He had hesitated this long. What was one more night? Tonight, he would think about what he was going to say. When he begged Merry's forgiveness and asked her to marry him, the words had to be exactly right.

Chilly and damp, Saturday suited Merry's mood. She stayed in bed until noon, something she hadn't done for years. After that, she made it to the couch. All her energy was concentrated on waiting for the phone to ring.

She had been waiting all week, hoping Sam would come to his senses, call her and apologize. Or at least let her know if he had reached some kind of decision. For the first time in her life she identified with the politicians who waited for the returns to come in from the polls. She'd waged a good campaign, but would it be enough to win?

She knew one thing. She wasn't going to run to Sam. From the very beginning, she had done most of the pursuing. This time it was definitely his turn. Not that she hadn't been tempted to call him. She had reached impulsively for the phone several times. But no. For once she was not being hasty. Maybe that was one thing she had learned from Sam—how to think before acting. She would be patient. And if Sam never called, she would...

Would what? she asked herself. Without Sam, she just didn't have any plans.

He doesn't love me enough, she told herself, shivering under her thin afghan. *If he loved me we could work through anything. With enough love we could juggle my career, the farm, our relationship and the kids. If only he loved me enough.*

Her nightmare had returned last night. Slightly different in form, as always, but just as frightening. Maybe more so. Familiar monsters can be the scariest of all, she thought, and the Sam in her dream was more monster than man, with blue eyes that shattered and cut into her heart.

The shrill scream of the telephone sliced through her pondering. She jumped, grabbing for the receiver, answering quickly.

"Merry?"

It was Sarah. Merry closed her eyes. She'd been trying not to think about the children.

"Merry?" Sarah repeated.

"Yes, I'm here."

"I'm scared."

Merry's eyes flew open. "What's wrong?"

"Aunt Beth is sick."

Calmly Merry told herself that Sarah's imagination could make a deathbed scene out of a headache. More than likely this was a ploy to get Merry out to the farm. The child could be a convincing little actress when there was something she wanted. "Where's your Daddy, Sarah? Or Jared? Can I talk to them?"

"Nobody's here but me and Aunt Beth. And she's in Daddy's room. She won't let me in, Merry."

Genuine alarm jangled along Merry's nerves. "Are you sure she's sick, Sarah? Sometimes people just want to be by themselves."

"No! She's sick, Merry. She's been acting funny ever since this morning." The child's voice caught on a sob. "I'm scared."

"Where did your Daddy go?" Merry asked.

"Somewhere with Jared and Uncle Bill. They've been gone all day."

Merry sighed with frustration. There was a chance that Beth really was sick. Just as there was a chance this was one of Sarah's little tricks. But Merry didn't believe in taking chances with people she loved. If something was wrong with Beth, then Sarah needed her.

"I'll be right there," she promised.

Hustling into some jeans and an old sweatshirt, she grabbed her bag. The sensible thing to do would be to call the paramedics, but that would only cause embarrassment if this was a false alarm. With Beth, embarrassment was the last thing Merry wanted.

At the farm, Sarah came running out into the rain to meet her, tears streaming down her face. The tears were convincing. The locked door to Sam's room was more so. The sounds Merry heard from inside clinched it, especially since she couldn't get Beth to answer her. The whole situation had the earmarks of a first-class nightmare.

Not knowing what she would find on the other side of that door, Merry sent Sarah to the barn, with instructions to wait until someone came for her. Then Merry set about trying to pick the lock.

Thankfully Aunt Eda Rue's house had boasted the same kind of old-fashioned doorknobs as the farmhouse. A frantic search turned up a bobby pin in one of the kitchen drawers, and with experienced ease, Merry got the door open.

Beth screamed when she saw Merry. Drenched in sweat and clutching at her stomach, the woman rose from the side of the bed and tried to walk. "No! Get out of here. I don't want you here!"

The sight Beth presented, eyes blazing in her pale face, momentarily shocked Merry into silence. She'd seen eyes like this before—half-crazed with pain and fear and hate, but she never thought she would see a gaze like this directed at her.

But Merry still had to help Beth. She grabbed her arm and tried to ease her back down on the bed. "What in God's name are you doing?"

Fist raised, the woman fell against her. Merry deflected the blow and caught Beth's full weight. They fell against the bed, and the edge of the foot rail dug into Merry's back as she cushioned the other woman. But Beth screamed again. Doubling over, she slipped to the floor, obviously racked by the pain of a contraction.

Instantly Merry was beside her. "Dammit, Beth, why have you been hiding in here?"

The pain passed, Beth threw off Merry's hand and weakly backed up against the bed. "Get away from me."

"Beth, let me help you—"

"No! You're not going to kill me, not like you killed Liza."

"What do you mean?"

"You heard me. You killed Liza! You know you did, so don't bother to deny it."

Even considering the woman's state, the words stung, and Merry denied them. "I didn't kill your sister—"

"Damn you, you did!"

Arguing was a pointless waste of time, especially since Beth and her baby needed medical attention right away. Grasping Beth's arm again, Merry asked, "How long have you been having contractions? Why haven't you called your doctor?"

Another scream tore from Beth as her body twisted from the force of another contraction.

And real concern cut through Merry. At this rate, the baby could be almost here. Barring complications, of course. Barring everything that could go wrong even under the best of conditions. With pains this close there wasn't going to be time to get Beth to the hospital. Somehow Merry had to get her calmed down. She was going to have to deliver this baby herself.

Merry took a deep, calming breath. "Listen to me," she said, giving Beth's shoulders a fierce little shake. "If you don't pull yourself together, you're going to lose your baby. Do you understand me?"

"No! You're not getting my baby!" Beth yelled, kicking out with her legs.

"Listen to me, Beth. I can help you."

Beth's eyes were glazed with fear, and she shrank away from Merry. "No! You killed Liza."

Summoning all her professional calm, Merry took hold of Beth again. "Stop thinking about Liza! This isn't the same—"

"But you stole Jared and Sarah from me, too."

So that's what she thinks, Merry said to herself. It certainly explained part of the woman's attitude these last few months. She tried to soothe her. "I didn't steal them, Beth. They love you. They'll always love you."

"No! You stole them. But you're not getting my baby. You're not—" The last words ended on a scream so piercing that Merry, who thought herself immune to the pain of childbirth, cringed in horror.

Then she collected herself again. She could think of only one way to break through Beth's incoherence. Merry slapped Beth's face—just as Sam appeared in the doorway.

Sam had heard Beth's last irrational words. He could see she was out of her mind with pain and fear. But still, it was a shock to see Merry slap her. "What in the hell are you doing?" he demanded, hurrying across the room.

"What does it look like?" Merry snapped. "She's having the baby, and I'm trying to get her to listen to me."

"It's a month too early for the baby," Sam said, pointlessly he realized. What did that matter now?

"Make her stop," Beth pleaded, reaching for him. "Make her stop, Sam. Go get Bill. Where's Bill?"

Merry looked up. "Yes, where is Bill? Maybe he can help us calm her down."

"I left him and Jared at an auction." Sam didn't bother to explain that he'd come home early to go talk with Merry. He had stopped at the farm to change. "I'll go make a call. We'll get Bill here—"

"No, don't leave," Beth pleaded, clutching at Sam's hand. "Don't leave me alone with her!"

"There's no time to get Bill," Merry cut in. "I don't

know how long she's been like this. Sarah called me half an hour ago.''

"Sarah?'' Sam looked around in alarm.

"She's in the barn,'' Merry explained. "Right now we've got to get Beth onto this bed. And you've got to convince her to let me help her.''

Sam didn't wait for further explanations. Quickly he knelt beside Beth. She didn't fight him, and he was able to get her onto the bed while Merry ran for her bag and called for an ambulance. He calmed Beth down long enough to allow Merry to examine her. Then she was hysterical again.

"I'm so scared,'' Beth gasped, tears streaming down her face. "I've been so scared for so long. I know I'm going to die, Sam.''

"No, you're not,'' he soothed, pushing her hair back from her forehead.

"Just like Liza—''

"You're not Liza.''

"I've known I was going to die ever since I found out I was pregnant. I don't want to die, Sam, I don't—'' Her words were cut off as she bore down on another pain, gripping his hand with a force that hurt.

Sam's worried glance met Merry's.

Her expression was grim. "The baby's almost here. But she's got to cooperate with us.''

"All right.'' Sam squared his shoulders and turned back to Beth. "Did you hear that? You've got to help. If you don't, your baby is going to die.''

"It's Merry—''

"Merry has nothing to do with it,'' he said harshly, shaking her. "Just look at me. Listen to me. Do what I say.'' The words must have finally sunk in, because some of the terror left Beth. She stopped struggling and centered her gaze on Sam's face.

After that, it seemed to Sam that the minutes bled together. Beth was in hard labor, but somehow he found the words to keep her calm. She began to follow the crisp instructions he relayed by way of Merry. She pushed down with the contractions and breathed in between. With her cooperation, the baby came quickly.

The wail of the ambulance siren cut through the air just as Merry placed a tiny, red-faced baby on Beth's stomach. "Look at this, Beth," Merry murmured, a look of wonder on her face. "A little boy—with all his fingers and toes."

To Sam's astonishment the two women smiled at each other. With what had transpired between them that smile seemed as much a miracle as the baby. The sight of her son certainly calmed Beth. She looked almost serene.

But it was Merry who held Sam spellbound. Through the whole ordeal, no matter what insults Beth had thrown at her, she had remained calm and in control. He had never loved her more than he did at this moment.

But there wasn't time to tell her. For Beth was pale and trembling, and Merry's jubilance had changed to concern.

"Sam, get those paramedics in here," she bit out. "I think Beth's going into shock."

Chapter Twelve

Later that afternoon Merry stood alone on the back porch, reliving those last tense moments with Beth. Under the circumstances, shock wasn't the worst thing that could have happened. Merry mentally ran down the list of possible complications. What if the baby hadn't started breathing normally? What if she'd had to perform a cesarean? What if...

"And the what-ifs will drive you crazy," she murmured, quoting Aunt Eda Rue. Merry folded her arms across her chest and took a deep breath.

The important thing was that Beth had survived. The baby, bless his hardy little soul, was fine, too. Merry closed her eyes and breathed a small prayer of gratitude that everyone, including her, had made it through the ordeal.

She'd had a few weak moments, though. Merry didn't like admitting it, but the adrenaline that had kept her going had almost failed a couple of times. She had called on every ounce of training and discipline to finish the delivery. In the back of her mind there had been this little voice that kept saying, "Beth can't die, too. Not like Liza. You'll never have any peace if you lose her or the baby." Over and over those words had drummed, blocking out Beth's insults, even Sam's calming voice. Those words had pulled Merry through.

Afterward the paramedics had hustled Beth and the baby to the hospital where her doctor was waiting. Sam had followed in his truck. A neighbor had brought Bill and Jared home. Bill had rushed to the hospital. And Merry had stayed behind with the children. They had been full of questions, but Merry had finally settled them in Jared's room with a game. Then she'd come out to the porch to collect her thoughts. Only a few hours had passed since Sarah's frantic phone call, but it felt more like days.

So much about Beth's behavior during the last few months made sense now. That she might have been afraid of dying in childbirth was somewhat understandable, given what had happened to her sister. The fear had been complicated by Merry's presence. Some twist of the mind or shift of hormones had convinced Beth that Merry had killed her sister and stolen the love of Jared and Sarah. Today, faced with premature labor, something in her had just snapped.

Trying to shake off the memory of Beth's hate-filled eyes, Merry again took a deep breath of fresh air. A fine, spring rain was falling, dripping from the eaves, splashing on the untidy row of shrubbery beside the porch. It was a farmer's favorite kind of rain, the slow and steady sort that seeps into the ground and makes things grow. The sound was soothing.

Everything Sam had once told her about spring on this farm was true. Even on this gloomy afternoon the landscape was full of color—the dark green of the lawn, the rich black soil of the plowed fields and the spots of soft purple where violets were blooming. The scents were just as he had described them, too—clean, fresh and fertile.

God, how she loved it here. Merry didn't want to leave this farm, just as she didn't want to leave Sam. He would have a fight on his hands if he expected her to go. She loved him, and she wasn't walking away just because the road had gotten a little rocky.

Planning her arguments, Merry waited on the porch for Sam. When his truck pulled up in the drive, she squared her shoulders, ready for the challenge.

"How's Beth?" she asked as he came inside.

"Doing fine." Sam was surprised to find Merry waiting for him here. Though he had rehearsed exactly what he was going to say all last night and on the way home, just seeing her sent the words right out of his head. All he really wanted was to hold her. Because he needed to do something with his hands, he shrugged out of his windbreaker, scattering raindrops to the floor of the porch. He stood looking at the puddle that had collected at his feet.

Stunned, Merry looked down, too. The puddle was just like in her dream. She glanced up, almost expecting Sam's eyes to shatter. They didn't, of course. But they were a deep, deep blue and filled with an emotion she couldn't quite fathom. She stood staring at him, not realizing for a moment that he was talking to her. "Pardon me?" she said, blinking.

"I said that Beth and Bill Jr. are doing great."

Merry had to smile at the appropriate name. The little scrapper who had been in such a hurry to enter the world was his father in miniature.

"Dr. Hughes said to let you know you did a super job," Sam added.

"It would have been much more difficult without your help."

"I don't know about that—"

"No, really. I was starting to get worried when you—" Though she fought it, Merry's voice broke on the last word.

And Sam's arms closed around her. "Thank God you were here," he murmured against her hair. "I'm so sorry about all the things Beth said. She took all her fear and anger out on you."

Though leaning on his strength was exactly what she wanted to do, Merry drew away. "Sam, Beth needs some help."

"I know, I know," he soothed, stroking his knuckles across her cheek. "I talked to Bill and to her doctor about that, too. I called her parents, and they're coming in from Arizona."

"That's fine, but she needs professional help."

"She's going to get it."

Merry sighed. "I hope she'll be okay, Sam. I mean, with the baby safely here, her worst fears should be over. If she gets some help, I bet she'll be just fine."

"I'm sure she will," Sam agreed, and then paused for a moment. "I wish I had realized how she felt. Maybe I could have helped her. I could have figured it out."

"You can't blame yourself."

"But I knew she never really got over Liza's death. I never even saw her cry. She was strong for everyone else—"

"The way women usually are," Merry agreed.

He caught her hands in his. "You were strong today."

"I was doing my job. Beth needed—"

"I don't want to talk about Beth anymore," Sam whispered as he started to pull her back into his arms.

She resisted. "Good, because I want to talk about us."

"I do, too," he interrupted. "I've been—"

Merry ignored him and forged ahead, anticipating resistance all the way. "You're not getting rid of me, Sam Bartholomew. Whatever the problems are, we can make it through them."

"I agree."

She blinked in surprise. Agreement was the last thing she had expected.

All of Sam's carefully rehearsed speech was forgotten as he continued, "I've been a stupid, bullheaded fool—too afraid of failure to listen to what you've been saying to me all along. I just couldn't see past the differences between us, Merry. I thought they would tear us apart."

"But—"

"I know, I know," Sam said, silencing her protest. "We've got plenty of things in common—especially love." His voice grew rough with emotion. "And I do love you, Merry Conrad. There was never any doubt about that." If his words had left any doubt in her mind, Merry thought his dazzling smile would have been convincing enough. Would she ever get enough of that smile?

Happiness can make you just as dizzy as fear does, Merry discovered. And for the second time that day she was assailed by weakness. Thankfully Sam was there for support, and the touch of his lips against hers was as effective as smelling salts.

But she still had some questions, and she pulled away to ask them. "What made you realize you were being a 'stupid, bullheaded fool'?"

"I started thinking about what my life would be like without you."

"How would it be?"

"Completely empty."

"I know the feeling," Merry whispered. "I didn't know what I was going to do without you."

"You could have taken that job in Kentucky," Sam said, only half teasing.

Merry's arms crept around his neck. "I turned down that job offer for good this week."

"I was afraid you wanted that job."

"I was afraid you wanted me to take it and get out of

your life.'' Merry laughed, realizing how stupid both of them had been. ''I thought I wasn't exactly the kind of person you wanted to share your life with.''

''There was never any problem with you,'' Sam said. ''What made you think such a thing?''

''Because I'm nothing like Liza.''

''Beth was the only one who said you had to be.''

''She only confirmed my own feelings of inadequacy.'' At Sam's puzzled look, Merry tried to explain. ''My work is so demanding. I can't be here all the time, for you or the kids. I'll always be missing things like the dinner I missed with Sarah.''

''We can get through stuff like that. As long as you eventually come home I don't care how long you have to stay at that hospital.''

''You may regret those words.''

He shook his head. ''No, I won't. Because I wouldn't change one thing about you. What you do is part of who you are, and I think you're the most beautiful, exciting woman in the world.''

Blinking away tears, she smiled. ''I'm going to need to be reminded of that from time to time, especially when I've been up all night with some baby demanding to be born.'' Her smile faded then. She had to make Sam understand how much she loved him. ''I need you, Sam. I need your strength and your love. Those things mean more to me than money or fancy houses or cars.''

Sam paused briefly to wonder why he'd had so much trouble believing her before. Now he knew for certain he had everything she required for happiness. He was going to make sure she stayed happy—for the rest of their days. Part of his carefully rehearsed proposal came back to him then, and he smiled down at her. ''I think we've wasted too much time, don't you?''

''Way too much,'' she agreed.

His voice deepened with emotion. ''So how about it, Dr.

Conrad, do you think you might want to marry this stubborn farmer?''

"Oh yes," she whispered, brown eyes shining. "Oh yes!" His kiss swept her so hard against him that her feet left the floor.

"Hey, guys, cut it out."

Pulling away from Sam, Merry's eyes met Jared's. The smile on his face belied his disapproving tone, and she smiled back.

"We're starving," Sarah announced, hands on hips, as she joined her brother in the doorway to the kitchen.

"Give me and Merry five more minutes, and then we'll go out for dinner," Sam promised.

That wasn't good enough for his daughter. "Oh, Daddy, come on."

"Just shut up, peewee," Jared taunted her. "Dad said five minutes."

"Daddy, Jared's callin' me names again!"

"You're such a baby—"

The familiar beginning of a Jared-Sarah battle receded a little as Sam kissed Merry again. Then he murmured, "Are you sure you really want a permanent spot in this family circus?"

The argument was like music to Merry's ears. The tender look in Sam's eyes was enough to make up for every disappointment she had ever known. Finally she wasn't on the outside looking in. She really did belong.

"I wouldn't trade *our family circus* for anything on this earth," Merry whispered, drawing Sam's lips back to hers. "For the first time in my whole life, I've got everything I want."

* * * * *

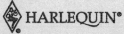

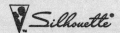

Please address questions and book requests to: Harlequin Reader Service U.S.: 3010 Walden Ave.,
P.O. Box 1325, Buffalo, NY 14269 CAN.: P.O. Box 609, Fort Erie, Ont. L2A 5X3

PAHGEN

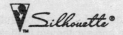

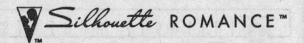

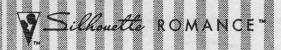

What's a single dad to do when he needs a wife by next Thursday?

Who's a confirmed bachelor to call when he finds a baby on his doorstep?

How does a plain Jane in love with her gorgeous boss get him to notice her?

From classic love stories to romantic comedies to emotional heart tuggers, **Silhouette Romance** offers six irresistible novels every month by some of your favorite authors!

Such as...beloved bestsellers **Diana Palmer, Stella Bagwell, Sandra Steffen, Susan Meiner** and **Marie Ferrarella,** to name just a few—and some sure to become favorites!

Silhouette Romance—always emotional, always enjoyable, always about love!